Enter Second Murderer

Set in Victorian Edinburgh, *Enter Second Murderer* is a novel of crime and detection in the classical tradition. The events which decide Detective Inspector Faro to re-open the sensational case of 'The Gruesome Convent Murders' (for which one murderer has already been executed) lead him into a bewildering labyrinth of passions, betrayal and greed concealed behind the lace curtains and respectable middle class exteriors of Edinburgh society

The bizarre list of prime suspects includes a fanatical nun, an aristocratic hermit, a schoolboy from the nearby public school and even a colleague of Faro's in the Edinburgh City Police is not above suspicion: all might have good reason for silencing the convent's second murder victim: the lovely, exotic and amoral Lily Goldie.

Faro finds light relief and fleeting romance among the Trelawney Thespians, while he re-examines and unravels the almost forgotten clues which conceal the identity and motive of the second murderer. Danger is never far away and Edinburgh's other face, that shady world of ever-erupting violence, threatens to engulf his own household. Unperturbed, his step-son, Vince, is determined that his newly acquired medical knowledge allied to Faro's powers of logic and deduction will prove irresistible in the detection of crime and the apprehension of murderers.

Alanna Knight is well known for her historical novels and non-fiction work. *Enter Second Murderer*, the first of a projected series featuring Inspector Faro, is a taut, exciting mystery and a very satisfying read.

Alanna Knight

ENTER SECOND MURDERER

An Inspector Faro Novel

MACMILLAN
LONDON

Copyright © Alanna Knight, 1988

First published in 1988 by
MACMILLAN LONDON LIMITED
4 Little Essex Street London WC2R 3LF
and Basingstoke

Associated companies in Auckland, Delhi, Dublin,
Gaborone, Hamburg, Harare, Hong Kong, Johannesburg,
Kuala Lumpur, Lagos, Manzini, Melbourne, Mexico City,
Nairobi, New York, Singapore and Tokyo.

British Library Cataloguing in Publication Data

Knight, Alanna
  Enter second murderer.
  I. Title
  823'.914[F] PR6061.N45

  ISBN 0-333-47013-3

Typeset by Matrix, 21 Russell St., London WC2

Printed and bound in England
by Richard Clay, Chichester, Sussex

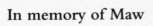

In memory of Maw

CHAPTER ONE

Patrick Hymes was tried and convicted at the High Court of Justiciary in Edinburgh for the murders of Sarah Gibson (or Hymes) and Lily Goldie. He made his exit from the world on 11 May 1870, a day that promised to be bright and cheerful for everyone but him. With the noose about his neck, to the accompaniment of a single blackbird's tumultuous song and without a single human tear as requiem, he went into eternity protesting his innocence of the second murder.

There was little known about Patrick Hymes, an Irish labourer whose pretty young wife had abandoned him and their two small children to make a new life for herself as maidservant in an Edinburgh convent. There the nuns were ignorant of her moral lapses, for Sarah Hymes was, in the parlance of the day, no better than she should be.

Patrick Hymes, a simple uneducated man, showed remarkable industry and ingenuity in tracking down his runaway wife, and luring her out for an evening stroll on the pretext of a reconciliation gift. He knew that baubles were the one way to Sarey's grasping heart. When his attentions threatened to become more familiar, as was his right, they quarrelled. His manly pride insulted, his role of husband and father belittled, Patrick dispatched Sarey by strangulation on the highest ridge of Salisbury Crags.

Hymes had, according to evidence at the trial, hoped to escape justice by her demise being classified as an unfortunate accident on a narrow path in an area notoriously prone to landslides. Even a cursory post-mortem examination, however, revealed suspicious marks of violence upon her person and bruises about her throat.

There was enough evidence in the subsequent murder of Lily Goldie, in similar circumstances, to convince everyone that she had also been the victim of Patrick Hymes. According to the newspapers, townsfolk were afraid to sleep in their beds at night.

'GRUESOME CONVENT MURDERS' ran the headlines, promising an epidemic of horrible strangulations. The police were assisted in their enquiries from a totally unexpected quarter: the troubled conscience of Patrick Hymes, who appeared all atremble at the Central Office of Edinburgh City Police and dramatically confessed to his late wife's murder. On producing proof of identity and evidence to link him with the murdered woman, there were sighs of relief all round. But even as the report was being hastily written in the Central Office, came the assassin's vehement denial.

'Lily Goldie? Who's Lily Goldie? Never heard of *her*.'

The evidence was read to him. Only two days earlier, the body of Lily Goldie had been discovered at the foot of Salisbury Crags, some hundred yards from the spot where Sarah Hymes was murdered. A remarkable coincidence made even more remarkable by the fact that she too had been strangled, not manually but with a scarf knotted about her neck. And stretching coincidence to its utmost: Lily Goldie was also employed, as a teacher, at the Convent of the Sisters of St Anthony in the Newington area.

Hymes was now eagerly accepted as Lily Goldie's slayer and sternly advised to admit to both murders and thereby make it easier for himself. Hymes continued to be outraged by the suggestion, expressing himself in violent language which was subsequently monitored for the ears and eyes of those with more sheltered upbringing as, 'I don't care what she was or who she was. I never heard of her. You find out who done her in – it weren't me.'

Resisting pleas that another confession would make a lot of people happy, and ignoring assurances that swinging for two murders was no more painful than swinging for one, he shouted, 'Easier for meself, you mean easier for yous. Ties it up all neatly.' And stabbing a finger at the unfortunate constable taking down his statement, 'You can write that in your — evidence.'

Refusing to be cajoled or threatened, Hymes remained stubborn on the matter of Lily Goldie.

For Detective Inspector Jeremy Faro, the case of Patrick Hymes, double murderer, meant a few less illusions about a depraved humanity, one more in the annals of sordid domestic crimes he had investigated during his twenty years with the Edinburgh Police Force.

On the eve of Hymes's dramatic confession Faro unfortunately had been struck down by a typhus-like illness, not altogether rare in Edinburgh City and with consequences fatal for those of less robust constitution than his own.

His stepson, newly graduated Dr Vincent Beaumarcher Laurie, had returned home to find him lying on the floor writhing with pain. The most cursory examination revealed a condition too advanced to respond to home treatment. Hailing a passing gig, he rushed Faro into hospital for immediate and drastic treatment.

Faro was grateful. He knew that he owed his life to Vince's presence of mind and the great good fortune of his leaving Dr Kellar's surgery earlier than usual that afternoon.

Vince had watched over him until he was out of danger, and as soon as he was able to return home again had questioned him closely. Had any of his colleagues suffered in a similar fashion?

That had been Faro's first question to his visitors from the Central Office. Heads were shaken, but Vince refused to be convinced.

'It is as I suspected, Stepfather. Someone was trying to get rid of you. Someone who had it in for you.'

'What an idea. I am hardly that important.' Faro laughed weakly. 'More likely one of Mrs Mallet's mutton pies, from the shop we patronise at the Central Office, was the culprit.'

The illness left him weak in body, depressed in spirits. Much as he disliked leaving a case before the trial, he felt too sick to protest. Suddenly the detective's long hours, where strong legs and stronger stomachs were absolute necessities, palled on him. Vince insisted that he must go away and convalesce, a suggestion received by Superintendent Mackintosh of the Edinburgh City Police with more than his usual warmth. Patting Faro's shoulder heavily, he said, 'You are too valuable to lose, Faro. Take a holiday, you deserve it. Why not go home for a while – as long as you like,' he added, with unaccustomed generosity.

Home was Kirkwall, in the Orkney Isles, where his two little daughters, Rose and Emily, aged eight and six, had lived with their grandmother since Lizzie died.

'Absolutely not,' said Vince. 'Much too far for you to travel – and a rough crossing is the last thing you need in your condition. Don't even consider it. Besides, you know how Grandmama fusses. How about your Aunt Isa? Her nursing experience would be admirable.'

Aunt Isa, nanny to several generations of middle-class children, had married a gardener at Balmoral Castle. A widow for many years, she lived in an estate cottage at Crathie, where Deeside's fresh air and some excellent fishing aided Faro's recovery better than the abundant good food, which still revolted him. Edinburgh and the existence of violent murder seemed remote as the moon and stars, impossible among those peaceful hills, and he hoped all would be resolved before his return.

He found instead that Hymes, his execution imminent, had made a last request to speak to Inspector Faro.

Faro went reluctantly, arriving at the cell as the priest was leaving. He had never overcome his distaste for the barbaric biblical law of an eye for an eye, a tooth for a tooth and a life for a life, especially in the case of a man who, far from being an habitual criminal, for one instant in his life lost control over man's most primitive emotion.

As he sat opposite Hymes, he felt sure he was right. There was something about a killer's eyes, a destroyer who kills wantonly, a quality that defied words but which his intuition told him was lacking in the man before him.

'You're a fair-minded peeler, I'm told. And as sure as God is me witness, I am no cold-blooded killer of innocent women,' said Hymes desperately. 'I killed my Sarey. That I freely admit and am willing to swing for the faithless whore that she was. The world is well rid of her. But that other lass – whatever they say, I never even laid eyes on her, much less a hand. Sure, it's a pack of lies they're pinnin' on me. Someone's made it look as if I done her in too. They needn't have bothered – I swing tomorrow – I've made my confession, I've received absolution for my crime and I'm not sorry to be quit of this world. I loved my Sarey and I'll love her with my dying breath – aye, and curse her in it too. But I'd never killed that other one.' He looked around the tiny cell, wild-eyed.

'Listen to me, Inspector. What I'm saying is the truth. Sarey would be alive if I hadn't a temper on me, always in me nature to be a violent man but only with her on account of her wicked nature. When we went out walking, so peaceful and agreeable like it started, I thought I could talk her round to coming home with me, back to our two poor bairns. But, Jezebel that she was, she laughed at me, scorned and cursed me, and when I tried to shake some sense into her, no different than I've done a score of times afore, I ended up with me hands around her throat, throttling the bitch.'

11

Hymes paused, looking at his hands spread out before him on the table as if he could not believe that they had performed the monstrous task. 'I don't remember anything till I heard her choking – the next moment she'd gone such a funny colour. Dear Mother of God, be merciful to me,' he whispered, and, laying his head on his folded arms, he sobbed.

'I didn't know she was dead, I swear it. It's just like I told you the first time when I gave meself up. I was that shocked I let go of her, as God's me witness, we were that near the edge of the path, she just went limp and rolled over the cliff on her own account. I've told them over and over. I never meant to kill Sarey, it was just an accident that could happen to any man on that narrow path.

'Not like that Lily, that strangling her with her scarf – now that was deliberate murder,' he added self-righteously as he waited, eager for some response from Faro, who could think of no words of comfort that were not either trite or inappropriate to the occasion. Faro could always put himself, however uncomfortably, into the criminal's shoes. What, he thought, if it had been my Lizzie? Would I not have experienced the same murderous rage of a husband and father betrayed, the same impulse to destroy? Since the labouring classes most frequently indulged in the pastime of wife-beating, murder often became violent chastisement that went too far. Such murders, Faro firmly believed, constituted no threat to the community, but the society who would share his humanitarian views was not yet born.

If the public who, ten years earlier, had rushed to see public executions, had seen and heard this pathetic emaciated wife-slayer (who bore little resemblance to the police-court drawings of a robust, fresh-faced labourer), they could never for a moment have believed that every female in Newington was in danger from such a creature.

Faro's silence was misunderstood. 'I see you don't believe

me, Inspector, either,' he said sadly, shaking his head. 'It doesn't matter for, even if you did, it can't change anything now. But God will believe me. He knows that murder's not in me nature and that I'm a peace-loving God-fearing man. Ask anyone who knows me two bairns, the good father that I am to them, denying them nothing, patient as a saint. Sure an' I know I'll go to hell for the cruel thing I did to Sarey and all the saints' prayers can't save me from the gallows tomorrow. But better to die than let Sarey destroy other happy homes and spoil men's lives like she did mine.'

There was an Othello-like dignity about the shabby little Irishman who had killed for love gone wrong, and despite the evidence of that second murder Faro had an unhappy feeling that he had listened to the truth and was assisting a miscarriage of justice, as well as ignoring the important and very disquieting implication raised by Hymes's protestations of innocence: the existence of a second murderer.

Returning to the Central Office, he took down the remarkably small packet which contained an account of the trial, and found that in retrospect the case made very curious reading. There were too many coincidences by far. From his long association with criminals, Faro suspected that the solution with Hymes as the double murderer was just a shade too convenient.

Superintendent Mackintosh, a man of large proportions with a voice like an army sergeant major, looked up from his desk. 'Seen him, have you? Still protesting, is he?'

'Yes. Frankly, I'm a bit uneasy about the whole thing. Doesn't it seem strangely out of character that Hymes should have murdered Lily Goldie? I mean, it was quite motiveless.'

'Motiveless? Of course it wasn't motiveless. The man's a damned villain. Totally unreliable. Can't expect people of that class to reason things out. Blood lust, that's what it was. His wife was a whore, so it follows that any woman

13

like her is a whore. Simple for anyone to understand that.'
And at Faro's doubtful expression, he thundered, 'Do you
know what you're suggesting, man?'

'I'm only suggesting further enquiries.'

'Further enquiries? You must be mad. Authority has to be
appeased and the public's demand for justice satisfied with
a hanging. And in the very unlikely event that Hymes didn't
murder Goldie, he still has to hang for the self-confessed
murder of his wife.'

'He claims it was an accident – manslaughter rather than
murder.'

Mackintosh banged his fist on the desk. 'Ridiculous,
Faro, the case has been tried and he's proved guilty and
that will have to satisfy you as well as everyone else.' He
paused. 'Are you suggesting that in your absence there
has been a miscarriage of justice?' When Faro was silent,
he said, 'You'll have to produce a second murderer.' And
jabbing a finger at Faro, he said, 'And you'll have a mighty
hard job doing that, I fancy. You won't get much help
from the police either, quite frankly, because any idea that
Hymes didn't kill Goldie puts forward the nasty suggestion
that we have failed in our duty and there's a murderer
still on the loose, roaming the streets of Edinburgh, with
other innocent lives – particularly young female lives – in
danger.'

With a clumsy attempt at placating Faro, he said, 'Be
reasonable, man. A public investigation, an admission of
what you suspect in the newspapers and there would be
chaos. You've been very ill, I realise. And you've had your
holidays. The High Court is almost into summer recess.
Sheriffs have families and domestic obligations too,' he
added plaintively.

Faro suppressed a smile, remembering that Mrs Mackintosh, though pint-sized, was a Tartar, who would not
hesitate to resort to husband-beating and similar violence
upon her husband, should he dare suggest cancelling or

delaying the annual family holiday at North Berwick.

Faro sighed. It was fairly obvious that such events, in the absence of the senior detective, had led to a hasty conviction which assumed that Hymes, in common with most murderers, was a consummate liar, who wished only to embarrass and perturb the police further and hamper their investigations.

'It's all there for you to read, Faro.'

Faro glanced at the papers. 'He doesn't bear much likeness now to the drawings. Did he ever look like this?'

Mackintosh shifted uncomfortably. 'Oh yes. But he was determined not to eat until he could get someone to believe his fantastic story. We didn't think force-feeding was called for in the circumstances – I mean, once he had been found guilty.' He smirked awkwardly. 'Seemed quite set on dying, although we tried to tell him that hanging's easier for a heavy man – takes a shorter time than for a light one.'

Faro cut short these unsavoury explanations. 'If, as you tried to prove, Lily Goldie was murdered because she had seen Hymes visiting the kitchen and had been a witness to the pair departing together for that last ill-fated walk on Salisbury Crags, why didn't she inform the police during the routine questioning which I conducted myself? She seemed baffled and shocked as everyone else at St Anthony's, her statement made no mention of lurking strangers.'

'Oh for heaven's sake, Faro. The man was found guilty. The case is closed. And you take my advice if you know what's good for you. Let sleeping dogs – and hanged murderers – lie.'

CHAPTER TWO

Faro walked briskly down the High Street, its eight-storeyed 'lands' looming above his head. This was market day and the noise of vendors, the yelling of fishwives in from Newhaven, the jostling of the crowds and the smell of hot, unwashed flesh were too much for him. Aware only that he was badly in need of some air, fresh and bracing, he hurried down past the Palace of Holyroodhouse. The romance and stormy passions lost for ever behind those grey walls never failed to move him, associated as they were with the story of his beloved Mary, Queen of Scots, beset by villains, tricked and cheated, betrayed. He often wished he had lived in those turbulent days and had been able to wield a sword in her name.

The noise of raucous bustling Edinburgh faded. Salisbury Crags, the distressing scene of the two murders, seemed to stare down at him reproachfully from its lofty heights. Quickening his steps beneath its grim shadow, he walked up the ancient Gibbet Lane towards his new home.

After Lizzie's death he had decided to remove himself from the more convenient house they had occupied in Cockburn Street. He needed a new beginning, and one day, walking in King's Park, he decided to take a look at Newington, which was rapidly developing as a popular suburb on the south side of Edinburgh.

The recently built villas lacked the splendid proportions and classical character of the New Town's Georgian

16

architecture and the house in Sheridan Place was too large and altogether too modern for his taste, having just managed to evade the gross exaggerations of the presently fashionable Gothic style, upon which curlicues and turrets ran rampant.

Faro had been captivated by the views from its windows. Arthur's Seat, Edinburgh's dramatic extinct volcano, filled the eastern skyline, the Pentland Hills, with their ever-changing light, drowsed in the west. By coincidence, the house's first tenant had been an elderly doctor, recently deceased. The fully equipped surgery on the ground floor suggested the benign workings of fate, that this would be the perfect home for Vince and himself. He considered himself unlikely to remarry and enjoyed the most harmonious relationship with his stepson, who would soon be setting up his own brass plate, once he had served his term as assistant to the police surgeon, Dr Kellar.

The house had the added attraction of a nearby gig-hiring establishment, in addition to one of the new horse-drawn omnibus services, very convenient for the Central Office in Parliament Square.

Perhaps most tempting of all, he had acquired with the house a modest but ready-made domestic staff: two kitchen-maids, who he decided were not at all necessary, and a housekeeper, Mrs Brook, who would be a great asset, especially as she had long and faithfully served the deceased doctor and was well acquainted with the rapidly growing Newington area.

Mrs Brook agreed with him on the matter of living-in maids and seemed anxious to dispense with this additional expense. Thus Faro settled happily in 9 Sheridan Place, a move he most urgently needed as a lifeline back into some semblance of lost family life.

'Ah, Inspector sir, the doctor was a widower, just like yourself.' And with a vigorous nod. 'Ye ken what it's like then, all too well. My late sir was right pleased wi' ma services. Came to him when the paint was just dry on the house – his poor wife was an invalid and I saw her through to the very end.' She sighed deeply. 'A melancholy life for a well-set-up gentleman like yourself,' she added with a slyly admiring glance, 'and that bonny young lad, too. Both of you surrounded by so many corpses. At least your last landlady didna' die on you, and that's a mercy.'

Faro was amazed that she knew so much of his history already and guessed that she had wheedled the story out of Vince, always eager for a gossip in her kitchen – an unfortunate trait which he would have to overcome in his chosen profession.

Mrs Brook had regarded him sympathetically. Not that she could blame any woman taking a fancy to the Inspector. Although she would have found it difficult to describe his features or his bearing exactly, beyond saying that he was tall and strong-looking, youngish still, with a good head of fairish hair and good features. 'Stern he is, but he can make a body laugh sometimes. Mind, ye'd no want to get on his bad side. He's no' the kind of man ye'd care to cross. He'd make a terrible enemy, that he would,' she whispered with an expressive shudder to her cronies, eager for more details.

And, flicking away invisible dust from the photographs on the mantelshelf, 'Have you no' thought of having these bonny wee lasses here with you?' And, with a sly look, 'Perhaps wi' them to take care of, we may expect another lady-wife in God's good time.' At Faro's expression, she realised she had gone too far and continued hastily, 'There are some nice schools . . .'

He hoped she wasn't about to recommend the convent school with its unhappy association with two recent murders.

'It's a weary life for those of us who lose a loved one. My own dear man has been gone these twenty years, but I still remember him in my prayers. We who have been spared should stick together.'

18

And stick together was quite plainly Mrs Brook's earnest intention. She talked too much and too often for Faro, who was of a somewhat taciturn disposition, but otherwise he hadn't any real objections. She was an excellent cook and an admirable housekeeper.

After Lizzie died, in those terrible weeks of disbelief and anguish that followed, he had been easily persuaded by his mother to let Rose and Emily remain with her in Kirkwall, in far-off Orkney. Mary Faro was a sensible woman. She had recognised her son's helplessness confronted by grief and the bewildering demands of two children under ten years old. Indeed, he seemed little more than a shocked child himself, this big strong man who could cope with violent crimes but when death knocked at his own door was found totally unprepared. His wounds must be allowed to heal before he was strong enough to resume the role of parenthood, and so he had moved into Leith with a remote cousin, a middle-aged spinster who ran a boarding-house. Her intentions were soon apparent. After the observation of the requisite period of mourning, she had expected to become the second Mrs Faro, a revelation which involved Faro in speedily removing himself to a safe distance.

Mrs Brook met him in the hall as he picked up his mail. 'Another wee postcard I see from Kirkwall,' she said with a sigh. 'Those bairns must miss their Da.' And, with a return to her favourite theme of absent daughters, 'There are always gentlefolk willing to act as governesses hereabouts.'

'My salary won't rise to private teaching,' said Faro, promptly disabusing Mrs Brook of any idea that detectives belonged to the wealthy classes. 'They are happy enough at their school mean time.'

'They have proper schools up yonder?'

Faro laughed. 'Indeed – and very good ones. I was educated there myself.'

Mrs Brook regarded this miracle with new respect. 'Well I never, Inspector sir, who would have ever thought that. You have come a long way, haven't you? Like that hamper— '

'Hamper?'

'Yes, Inspector sir. It arrived this morning by the carter and I got them to put it in your study.'

Faro recognised the hamper, which had belonged to his father. As Mrs Brook put it, Inspector Faro had come a long way. But perhaps not as far as Constable Magnus Faro, the Orkney-born policeman who had served with the Edinburgh Police Force in its earlier days. He had died in an accident, which his wife refused to believe was anything else but deliberate murder. Mary Faro had taken their only son back to her own people, never having got used to living in the city and wishing only to leave behind Edinburgh, which had held out so much promise for their future and had brought only bitter grief and sad memories.

Memories of his father for young Jeremy were far from sad. Possessed of remarkable and almost total recall, which was to prove invaluable in his profession, he could remember in vivid detail the father who had gone out of the house one morning, waving him goodbye, and had returned, carried into the house, cold and still on a bloodied stretcher that evening.

Jeremy had been four years old. But he was never to forget his father's stories of crimes solved and other baffling mysteries unexplained. These had so stimulated his childish imagination that, to his mother's surprise and much against her wishes, he had resolved early in life to make the police force his career. Later, he sometimes wondered whether hero-worship and stories from his mother had built an image that did not exist beyond the silhouette of the handsome policeman on the mantelshelf.

'There's the young doctor now,' said Mrs Brook, 'with another load for the washtub, I see. It's a good job I'm not queasy by nature, being as how I'm used to doctors. All that blood, turns a body's stomach.'

Faro watched Vince striding down the street. Corn-bright curls, deep blue eyes framed by black eyebrows and eyelashes, it was little wonder that the boy's presence was such a comfort, when his sweet Lizzie haunted him every day from out of her son's face. Vince was twenty-one. Lizzie had been but four years older, mother of a nine-year-old son, when they first met. Faro thought wistfully of the future and of his strange fancy that if Vince and he stayed together in this house until they too were old, then his dear wife too would remain with him, never lost, through the years.

The lad had inherited his mother's beauty without her gentle nature. In childhood, he had exhibited a will of iron combined with a violent temper. A nasty, truculent child, difficult for anyone to love, let alone a prospective stepfather. From the beginning Vince had made evident his dislike and disgust at his mother's choice of husband – and Lizzie had made many excuses, certain that being born with the stigma of bastardy had been the cause of it all. For her lapse, Lizzie had not been made to suffer in Skye as she might have done in a more Calvinistic city environment. Islands had sympathy for girls who got into trouble, especially fifteen-year-old servants in the laird's house who were seduced, or, more often, found themselves helpless against what amounted to rape, by rich callous guests.

Since the death of Lizzie and their newborn son, he had needed Vince, as all that remained to him of his beloved wife. From the unlikely spring of dislike and resentment, tolerance and friendship had sprung up between bereaved husband and son, as they sought forgetfulness in agreeable leisure activities, walking in the hills and canoeing on the River Forth. The only echoes of Vince's early rebel-lion shone forth in occasional lively and ill-timed student

21

pranks, which gave his policeman stepfather a somewhat red face. But Faro was proud indeed of the boy he now regarded as his own son in every way except the accident of conception.

Having made his escape from Mrs Brook, he retreated to his study upstairs, reproached by the loving message from Rose and Emily – saying that they had not had a letter from dear Papa for some time. Resolving to write immediately, he opened the other letter and drew out a head-and-shoulders photograph of a handsome young man: 'To my lovely Lily, Ever your T.'

The note enclosed was from the Mother Superior at the Convent of St Anthony.

> This photograph was found by one of the nuns when she was clearing out the room which had been occupied by the unfortunate Lily Goldie. It had presumably slipped down behind the skirting-board and had been overlooked during the police search. I realise that the case is closed but I thought you might like to add it to the unhappy girl's possessions which I understand are in police-keeping awaiting a claimant.

There had been no mention of 'T.' in the report on Lily Goldie's murder, of that he was certain. Was this new evidence in the case? With a sense of growing excitement, Faro carried the card to the window and was re-reading the letter from the Mother Superior when Vince's conversation with Mrs Brook in the hall announced his imminent appearance.

'Good-day, Stepfather. Caught any criminals today?'

Faro smiled at the boy's usual greeting. 'Not today, lad. I've just had a last interview with Hymes.'

'New evidence?'

Faro shook his head. 'No. Just the same old story, that he didn't murder Lily Goldie. I'm inclined to believe him, dammit.'

Vince was silent for a moment. 'You know my feelings, Stepfather. I think – although the good Doctor Kellar nearly had a fit when I suggested such a thing – I think that Lily Goldie was killed by the fall – doubtless she was pushed, and that scarf was tied around her neck, afterwards, to make it look like murder.'

'That's precisely what Hymes maintains.'

'Ah, but how do we prove it?'

'We can't, unless we produce a second murderer.'

'Or unless our second murderer strikes again. Talking of which, the Pleasance Theatre are putting on *Macbeth* this week. Shall I get you a ticket?'

'I don't know that I'm strong enough to see the Immortal Bard murdered by amateurs just now.'

Vince laughed. 'Don't be such a snob, Stepfather. They are professional actors: Mr Topaz Trelawney's Thespians. You've missed a very popular season and there are only two weeks left. You must see them, some of the actors are very good indeed, particularly the leading lady. She's an absolute stunner, probably Mrs T.,' he added regretfully.

Faro smiled. His stepson had a penchant for actresses, but usually of the more frivolous variety.

'Oh, talking of "T."— '

'What an outrageous pun, Stepfather.'

'I mean the initial "T." – have a look at this.'

Faro handed him the photograph and the note.

'Good Lord, I know who this is.'

'You do? Could this be our missing man – our second murderer?'

Vince shook his head. 'The likeness flatters him, but I'd swear it's Timothy Ferris. He was in my year at medical school.'

'Did he know Lily?'

'Oh yes, indeed. He met her in January when we all went skating together on Duddingston Loch. He was quite infatuated— '

'A missing suitor, by God. Now we're getting some-where,' said Faro excitedly.

'Only on the road that leads to the grave,' said Vince solemnly.

'What do you mean?'

'I mean that Tim is dead, Stepfather. By his own hand. Committed suicide, walked under a railway train.'

Faro remembered vaguely the case as just another of the tragic suicides that were encountered almost every day at the Central Office, routine investigations in which he wasn't concerned. Except to thank God it wasn't his son – or stepson – that had been driven to such an end. The asso-ciation with Lily Goldie put the matter of Timothy Ferris into new perspective. But the time-factor was wrong.

Vince nodded. 'Yes, he died two weeks before Lily's murder. Remember, I told you? He failed his last qualifying exams and was thrown out at the beginning of the term. He wasn't a particular friend of mine, but rumour had it that he was deeply involved with some girl who was leading him on.' And, picking up the photograph, 'That would fit the character of Lily.'

'What about his family?'

'Didn't have any. He was an orphan. However, he always had plenty of cash to spend on wine and gam-bling. Bit of a waster, was Tim. And there was a rumour of some rich relative supporting him through medical school.'

'I seem to remember you went to the funeral?'

A look of pain crossed Vince's face. 'It was at Greyfriars, Stepfather,' he said, trying to sound casual as for a moment they fell silent, remembering that other beloved grave, the mother and wife who was gone from them. 'I steeled myself,' Vince continued. 'Matter of courtesy, you know, from his year, when he had no relatives. We were the only mourners. No girls that I noticed. And I would have remembered Lily Goldie, especially as I had to assist at

24

the post-mortem, one of my first cases,' he added with a shudder. 'Bad enough having to deal with the corpse of a total stranger, but to encounter a pretty girl one has met before, even on the slightest acquaintance . . . I had nightmares.'

'Tell me again – about the post-mortem.'

'Nothing much to tell – a lot of bruising, a broken wrist and pelvis, and contusions which would be the case for anyone falling from a steep crag – either falling naturally or grappling with an assailant wouldn't make much difference by the time she reached ground-level. Those marks about her neck were very different from what you'd expect of a labourer's strong hands.'

'You suspected that the murderer followed her down to . . . ?'

'Exactly. And tied the scarf about her neck afterwards to make it look like Hymes's work. Unfortunately Doctor Kellar is a pig-headed gentleman and he laughed my idea to scorn. "Enthusiastic young amateur doctors mustn't let their personal interest in cases take precedence over good sense. One must learn to be dispassionate."

'I think he rather gauged by my reactions – since I was very sick at one point – that I had been infatuated with her.' Vince smiled grimly. 'Poor Lily, in life we had the most superficial acquaintance which would hardly have justified the intimacy of a post-mortem. Ironically, I found myself remembering her effect on the more susceptible of my year. Not that she wanted penniless students, she had her sights set well above the likes of us.'

He looked at Faro thoughtfully. 'You know, her tragedy was being born in the wrong age. She should have been a Nell Gwyn or a Pompadour, a courtesan, who knows no allegiance except to her own ambition. She must have been desperate indeed to seek employment in a convent. By the way, I've kept all the newspaper accounts about Hymes that you wanted.'

From behind the clock on the mantelpiece, Vince withdrew a small sheaf of newsprint. 'Let's see. "GRUESOME CONVENT MURDERS",' he read in mock sepulchral tones. '"Chills of horror are being experienced in the respectable modern Edinburgh environs of Newington and Grange where the brutal murders of two innocent female victims from the Catholic Orphanage of St Anthony have thrown a blight of fear and foreboding over sisters and pupils alike at the school whose activities are seriously affected."' He paused before continuing. '"Sufferings of extreme illhealth prevented the well-known and exceedingly brilliant Detective Inspector Faro from solving these interesting and diabolically wicked crimes."'

'Give it here – it doesn't say that.'

'Well, it should.'

'This one solved itself – thanks to Hymes's confession.' Faro sighed, with a shake of his head. 'Nothing more to do.'

Vince regarded him narrowly, very much the doctor. 'Feeling all right today, Stepfather? No more nasty griping pains? Appetite getting better?'

'I'm still a bit shaky, more easily tired than I should be, but with a kind of typhus that isn't surprising.'

Vince scratched his cheek thoughtfully. 'I still wonder, you know.'

'Wonder?'

'Yes. About your illness. I think you were deliberately poisoned.' Even when Patrick Hymes gave himself up, Vince stoutly defended his theory of a sinister plot to poison his stepfather. 'I must say, though, you're looking better every day. Still rather too thin, I fear. By the way, I met Constable McQuinn in Rutherford's howff – he was very solicitous about your health. When were you coming back? Were you fully recovered? Etcetera, etcetera.'

Faro felt annoyance return, the distaste for anything connected with Constable McQuinn, who had taken over

26

the Hymes case when Faro took ill and there was no other senior officer available. Now he felt as if being ill had played into Constable McQuinn's hands and a little responsibility had increased his bumptiousness and made him more know-all than ever.

Faro grunted and Vince smiled. 'You don't like the amiable constable much, do you?'

'No. He smiles too much and too often. Even when he's talking about a sudden death, you'd think he was laughing at a secret joke. And I get a nasty feeling that it's not so much my health as my job he's after. And he should have found that photograph of Timothy Ferris, too, in the final routine search of Lily Goldie's room. It was evidence, after all.'

'You're not going to complain about that, I hope,' said Vince anxiously.

'I'm not – but I'd be within my rights.'

'Come, Stepfather, you're being too hard on him.' Vince smiled. 'Don't worry. He's got a long way to go before he's had enough experience to be a threat to the job of detective inspector. Can't be much older than I am.'

Ignoring this plea to be reasonable, Faro decided that the photograph of Ferris presented an irresistible opportunity of putting the unctuous young policeman in his place.

Next morning he found Constable McQuinn sitting at his desk, smiling and whistling to himself, in a manner that suggested life was being very good to him. He yawned and shook his shoulders with a grin. Was he reliving the night's conquests, the unsuspecting serving girls and shop assistants who seemed to be his prey?

And approaching his desk, Faro wondered if he was seeing in the handsome young constable the youth he had never been. Was envy the root-cause of his irritation whenever he met McQuinn off-duty in Princes Street Gardens or listening to the band in the park, strutting like a

27

pouter pigeon with a different giggling young female on his arm?

At Faro's approach, he stood up, straightened his tunic and saluted his superior officer politely. 'A pleasure to have you back with us, Inspector. I trust you are fully restored to health again— '

'Never mind about that,' interrupted Faro ungraciously, and held out the photograph, carefully concealing the inscription. 'Have you ever seen this before?'

McQuinn looked thoughtful. 'Can't say as how I have, Inspector. Should I have seen it?' he added, smiling gently.

'Since it was discovered by one of the nuns in Lily Goldie's room, of which you were supposed to have conducted a thorough search, one would, in the normal way, have expected it to be produced along with any other evidence,' said Faro heavily, his temper rising.

McQuinn, refusing to be ruffled, held out his hand. 'May I?'

'Well, do you know who it is?'

McQuinn's smile was condescending to the point of insolence. 'Of course I know who it is. Everyone knows who that is, Inspector.'

'Then perhaps you'll oblige me— '

'It's Timothy Ferris, a suitor of Lily's.'

'Is that so? Then why wasn't this information produced in your report?' barked Faro, ashamed to hear echoes in his own voice of the bullying manner he so despised in Superintendent Mackintosh.

McQuinn sighed wearily. 'Inspector sir, seeing that the unfortunate young gentleman had committed suicide two weeks before Lily was murdered, even if we had found his photograph, such information would not have lent any relevance to the case.'

Looking at his superior officer's angry face, he continued, 'If you're in any doubt, all the details relating to Ferris's death are on file. Would you like me to fetch them out?'

'No, no.'

McQuinn nodded. 'May I suggest that you talk to your stepson? Ferris was in his year at medical school. Vince probably knows a great deal about his activities – by personal contact or hearsay from their fellow-students— '

Faro cut him short. 'Yes, yes.' And, somewhat angrily, he went over to the cupboard, unlocked it and, taking out the file on Lily Goldie, he threw in Ferris's photograph.

McQuinn watched him. 'So the case of Lily Goldie is finally closed, Inspector.' He sounded relieved.

'Is it? I wonder, McQuinn, I wonder.' And with that enigmatic reply Faro stalked out of the office and slammed the door behind him, harder than was completely necessary. In the corridor he stopped. Was that McQuinn's suppressed laughter he heard following him, or was it only his over-sensitive imagination?

CHAPTER THREE

The case of Hymes and the Gruesome Convent Murders was forgotten as an uncommonly hot dry spell of weather brought a spate of stomach upsets. There were people who complained that the weather was to blame, and mark their words there would be an outbreak of typhus if it continued. The same folk belonged to the order of gloomy prophets who foretold that every winter chill would also carry off half the population to the kirkyard.

No rain came, the skies remained obstinately blue and cloudless as handkerchiefs were pressed to noses by those forced to encounter the noxious odours emanating from narrow crowded city streets. An Edinburgh without rain was a phenomenon, especially as the mired stinking cobblestones relied upon frequent and heavy showers as Nature's way of keeping them fresh and clean.

Meanwhile, in Faro's garden, the lilacs had their day, to be replaced by an abundance of June roses. He could not fail to notice that their perfume competed with a distinct smell of faulty drains. He also observed, with considerable delight, a great deal of domestic activity in his back garden, where blackbirds and thrushes had nested, the proud male parent easing the wearisome egg incubation of a mate with a dawn and eventide song of joyous exultation.

Faro had little time to enjoy this novelty of his new home, happily distant from the city, for he was once again involved in the sordid crimes that lay behind the façade of city life.

Thefts, embezzlements, sexual assaults, child prostitution – such were mere scrapings on the surface which respectable, prosperous middle-class Edinburgh was at pains to present to the world. Deaths there were too, in drunken fights and street accidents, but none that bore any resemblance to the murders of Lily Goldie or Sarah Hymes.

At the end of a long day on a routine smuggling case at Leith Docks, Faro decided that, compared with the gruesome details of murder cases, there was something almost wholesome about cheating the revenue. Returning to the city, he saw that the radiant summer had temporarily disappeared in swirling mists which hid Arthur's Seat entirely and blotted out the Pentland Hills, but he felt strangely content as the omnibus set him down at the end of his street.

Glad to be returning home, he put his latchkey in the door and found Mrs Brook eagerly awaiting his arrival in order to announce a visitor.

'A lady to see you. I put her in the drawing-room. Said it was urgent, poor soul. I just couldn't turn her away.'

Faro swore silently, his elation suddenly abated. Tonight, for the first time since illness had deprived him of all appetite and interest in food, he was feeling hungry, looking forward to the evening meal as appetising smells of cooking drifted up from the kitchen. Dear God, a visitor was the last thing he wanted.

'Couldn't you have told her to come back tomorrow, got her to leave a message or something?' he demanded irritably.

'I hadn't the heart to send the poor lady away, Inspector sir. She'd come all the way from Glasgow on the train. And in a terrible state, poor thing. I don't know when she last had a good meal.' She lowered her voice with a glance towards the stairhead. 'Very ill, she is, Inspector sir, if I'm not mistaken. Fair wrung my heart just to look at her.'

31

Mrs Brook eyed his stony face reproachfully. 'I took the liberty of reviving her with a wee sup of your brandy, sir.' Leaning forward, she whispered confidentially, 'Have no fears, Inspector sir. A proper lady, she is. You know I would never let the other sort in – I mean to say, any person in who wasn't a gentlewoman.'

Faro tried to conceal his annoyance. As far as he was concerned, the good Mrs Brook had behaved like the busy-body she was proving to be, well-meaning, but a bit of a nuisance. In normal circumstances, he realised, he might have applauded her thoughtfulness, but not tonight, on the occasion of the resurrection of his lost appetite. He knew perfectly well that he was being selfish but the prospect of a stranger to deal with made him feel suddenly old and tired again, conscious of being footsore and with a childish need to be cosseted.

As if aware of her employer's conflicting thoughts, Mrs Brook began, 'I hope what I did was for the best— '

'Wait a minute – what did she want anyway that couldn't wait?'

At this sharp rejoinder, Mrs Brook gave him an almost tearful glance. 'I see I did wrong asking her in, sir. I'm sorry and I won't do it again. But – well, see for yourself. She's just lost her only brother, poor lady.'

'I don't see what I can do about that, Mrs Brook. This is a case for missing persons. Did you not tell her to go to the police?'

'She asked to see you personally.' Mrs Brook sounded offended. 'I expect she read about you in the newspapers. She said you were the only one who could help her.'

Faro sighed. 'What else did she tell you?'

'Nothing else. She was that upset, and I'm not one to pry,' Mrs Brook added, tightening her lips self-righteously.

A lost only brother? Cynically Faro thought that usually meant the brother or cousin was the polite term for a lover. If the woman upstairs was upset, that meant they had been living together and he had run off with someone else and most likely taken her money with him. So why ask for him? Thanks to Mrs Brook's compassion he'd have to listen to the whole wearisome story, utter platitudes of comfort and then get rid of her with some plausible excuse.

Mrs Brook took his rather curt nod as approval and beamed upon him. 'I'm glad I did right, Inspector sir.' She watched him walk upstairs, little guessing that where her employer was concerned her kind heart was likely to be her undoing. If it continued to interfere with her efficiency then she would have to go, Faro decided. He must make it plain to her that being housekeeper to a policeman needed sterner qualities than those for dealing with sick patients. After all, policemen were known to have strange callers, criminals, avengers, informers, and God only knew who she might let into the house through her ever-open, ever-welcoming kitchen door.

He opened the drawing-room door. At the bay window a woman reclined against the sofa cushions. At first he thought she slept, and his entrance did not disturb her. For a big man, Faro could move both swiftly and noiselessly. When he looked down on her, she opened her eyes and sat up with considerable effort.

One glance told Faro the reason for Mrs Brook's concern. The woman's face was pale, emaciated, exhausted-looking and ill beyond the mere travel-worn. Faro's quick eye for detail took in the shabby gentility of dress, the unmistakable badge of the lady's maid.

He closed the door behind him with the well-worn words, 'What can I do for you?'

As she tried to rise, both hands propelling herself forward, a fit of coughing took her.

As she struggled, trying to apologise, Faro said:

'Please, remain seated. My housekeeper tells me you have been ill. May I get you some refreshment to help?

My stepson is due home soon, he is a doctor – he may be able to offer you some restorative medicine.'

'No medicine can help me now, Inspector. But it is good of you to concern yourself.' She gave him a sad smile. 'I am quite beyond the reach of medicines now, I fear.'

Faro did not doubt that she spoke the truth, observing the two bright spots upon her cheeks, the bright eyes and flushed countenance of one far gone in consumption.

'I know I have taken an unpardonable liberty in visiting your home, instead of waiting to see you at the police office tomorrow. I was desperate, I thought you might be able to help me, for when I enquired they told me that the case is now closed.'

Faro was aware of a sick feeling that marked the return of his illness as observation of that skeletal face struck a chord: the emaciated Hymes in his prison cell. He asked what he already knew: 'What case is this?'

'I'm Maureen Hymes, Patrick's sister. I came over from New York hoping to see him. They let me see him, five minutes – five minutes, after all these years. Five minutes – before— ' Her voice ended on a sob, quickly controlled.

'Miss Hymes – er, that was a month ago.' He had not the heart to add, what was the point of coming to him now, whatever her reason.

'I know. I was ill. Afterwards – afterwards I went back to Glasgow. Pat had friends there. I collapsed.' She threw her hands wide. 'You can see the state I'm in, Inspector. They didn't want me to come to you, but I promised Pat. "If it's the very last thing I do, I'll prove that you didn't murder that Goldie woman," I told him at that last meeting. You see, Inspector, we were more than brother and sister, Pat and I were twins. Here's our birth certificate, if you're still doubtful.'

Born Cork, thirty-six years ago, Patrick and Maureen Hymes, he read.

34

'Things were bad in Ireland when we were children. The potato famine in forty-five, and then both our parents died. Patrick came over to Glasgow, eleven years old he was and he worked anywhere, at any kind of child labour that would pay well, to buy me a passage to America where we had an uncle. He thought I'd be safe there, have a decent life. One day he promised he'd save enough money to come over. When I got to New York, Uncle Paddy had died and his widow didn't want another mouth to feed.'

She stopped with a dismissive gesture. 'I won't be troubling you with the rest, Inspector, except to say that I went into service, bettered myself. Twice I made enough money to send to Patrick to fulfil his dream. Twice that money was stolen. God didn't intend us to meet again, but we wrote letters. I knew Sarah was a bad lot – he hinted at things in letters. He once said if anything happened to him, would I take care of his two little girls.'

She smiled wanly, looking out of the window, where the great bulk of Arthur's Seat glowed in a reflected sunset. 'I never told him how ill I was. I didn't want him to know. And then, when I heard – this terrible business – I sold everything I owned in the world to come and see my brother and fulfil my promise. Those two children have no one else in the world now. I have to see them provided for – find them good homes before I – before I die,' she ended firmly.

Faro was aware that, as she spoke, the Irish accent predominated the American. He was also increasingly aware of how strong the likeness must have been when the Hymes' were children, before the world's grosser sins took over her twin brother.

'I don't doubt that Sarah deserved to die,' she said. 'But I know that it was manslaughter rather than murder. And my Pat never killed that other girl. He's no deliberate murderer, that I do know, as God is my witness. You see, he never lied to me once in his whole life.'

She smiled. 'You might find this hard to believe, but Pat's great dream was to be a priest. That's what he was saving so hard for – and then he met Sarah. I suspect she seduced him and stole the money I sent. Anyway, he had to marry her with a bairn on the way. But he never lost his faith, he still lived by it.'

She paused, exhausted, breathing heavily. 'Inspector, you must take my word for it, someone else murdered that other girl and let Pat take the blame. I've got to find out the truth to save his immortal soul. And you've got to help me. You've got to – you're my last hope on earth of clearing my brother's name.' And she began to cry.

Faro stared at her, incredulous. And you've got to help me, she said. Just like that. What was she asking? That he had to prove a dead man innocent. And he wasn't even a Catholic. He was a lapsed Presbyterian. Maureen Hymes wasn't only sick, but mad, poor creature.

In his profession Faro found it a disadvantage to be susceptible to women's tears. Most men found them embarrassing, throat-clearing occasions, whereas Jeremy Faro, trained to the tears and supplications of two small daughters, had a natural inclination to enfold this delicate, child-like woman to his shoulder and comfort her.

'Do you believe in miracles, Inspector? I should, but I can't. But I do believe in dreams. And my brother haunts mine. You may be like all the others and reckon that a man who murders once will do so again, that he might as well hang for two as for one. But I know I'll be haunted to all eternity unless I can free him from the stigma of that other woman's murder.'

She stood up, faced him squarely. 'Now I must go. Thank you for listening to me so patiently, sir, and for giving me your precious time.' She paused, then shook her head. 'I'm sorry. I see I've failed to convince you.' She cut short his protests with a sudden dignity that again reminded him forcibly of the condemned man in his prison cell.

36

'Good evening, Stepfather. Oh – my apologies, I did not realise you had a visitor.'

It was Vince. Faro had forgotten that he too would be impatiently awaiting his supper, at the end of a long day in Dr Kellar's surgery.

Faro gave him a hard look, knowing that Mrs Brook, agog with curiosity about the mysterious woman who had suddenly appeared, must have sent him up post-haste to report on what was now taking place in the drawing-room.

As Faro made the introductions, Vince's eyebrows shot upwards at the name Hymes.

'This lady is his twin sister.'

Vince bowed over her hand, holding it now with an anxious, searching glance into her countenance that betrayed the doctor's interest.

'I have been a great nuisance,' she said, 'burdening the Inspector with my troubles. Your stepfather is a kind man and a very good listener.'

Vince's quizzical glance demanded explanation.

'Miss Hymes does not believe that her brother murdered Lily Goldie.'

'Indeed? Then if there was someone else, I can assure you, madam, my stepfather is just the man to hunt him down. He is marvellously clever, you know. No one could ever escape him for ever— '

'Steady on, Vince, I'm not infallible – and I cannot allow you to give Miss Hymes false hopes. The case is closed officially, remember.'

Vince made an impatient gesture. 'But if he does exist – this other murderer – then this is the very man for the job.' He pointed dramatically at Faro, the lamplight glinting on his pale hair, suddenly the picture of an avenging angel. 'Come now, there must be clues, Stepfather, and you are quite excellent on clues.'

Faro's reply was modest and non-committal. He was amazed amd moved that this boy, once so sneering, so wilful, even cruel on occasion, had vanished and left a gallant, caring and suddenly frighteningly vulnerable individual. Vulnerable – was that the word? Was this dropping of the scales from his eyes conditioned by familiarity, familiarity that had blinded him to the qualities of the man emerging from the chrysalis of youth, a man who would some day make a fine doctor – unless some day his vulnerability to defenceless womankind seriously affected his good sense?

'Where are you living in Edinburgh?'

'Nowhere. But I return to Glasgow to my – friends.' A bout of coughing cut her short again. She stood breathless, and Vince's solemn shake of the head in Faro's direction confirmed his worst fears.

'Then I will get a cab and see you safely to the railway station.'

'No – you are too kind, Doctor.'

'Not kind, Miss Hymes. It is my pleasure. I will be back directly.'

As Vince dashed downstairs and out into the street, Faro assisted his visitor to the front door. 'I should not have let him go to all this trouble. Please persuade him that I am perfectly capable of making my own – way.' Again she was shaken by the coughing that the slightest exertion seemed to bring about.

'Please give me your address.'

There was hope in her eyes as she opened her reticule and took out a slip of paper. 'I have it here. You will let me know . . .?'

The sound of wheels on the cobbled street announced the arrival of Vince and the cab. Together they assisted her inside, and Faro's last sight of Maureen Hymes was a frail hand raised in his direction, and lips forming the word, 'Promise . . . promise . . .'

As he closed the front door and walked slowly upstairs again, Faro realised that he had never before seen how his stepson reacted to a woman in distress, even a female long past thirty. He had rarely seen him in young female company, except as a boy at parties, bullying and tormenting small girls into screaming fits. Handsome he was, even then, but under that angelic appearance a frightful bully, who had never been asked to parties a second time. After all, few children are little angels, and he included his own dear Rose and Emily.

As he sat down and penned a loving response to their postcard, he was glad they had each other as comfort in their bereavement. Strange, although they adored each other now, Rose had been an extremely jealous two-year-old. When Emily lay newly born and rather raw-looking in her mother's arms, Rose had studied her carefully. 'She's not very pretty, is she? I like my dolls better than her. Can we send her back now, Mama?'

At least his daughters were the product of a happy and secure life. One day they would recover from the shattering grief of losing their mother. Born of their parents' wedded love, they had not suffered the stigma of bastardy which Vince had doubtless endured most painfully in his childhood. Even though his mother's little lapse was overlooked by the adult population, he imagined that the crofter children would not be ready to forgive so easily when they had the opportunity to hurt so cruelly. Doubtless Vince's difficult childhood had its roots in an ill-treatment he would be too proud to discuss with his mother.

When Vince returned, Faro looked at him gratefully. Thank God his fears – and Lizzie's – about the way the lad would turn out were ended. He only wished she could see her son now. How proud she would be of the man he had become.

'That was very good of you, lad,' he said as Vince followed him across the hall.

'It was the least I could do for a dying woman. Her life is now measured in days, hours, even, and I doubt exceedingly if she will reach Glasgow alive. She will certainly never return to Edinburgh.' He stood with his back to the blaze, since dining in a fireless room at the height of summer was unthinkable to Mrs Brook. 'A good blaze is as nourishing as a good meal' was one of her most frequent quotations.

The furniture which Faro had inherited with the house was handsome and mellowed with age and usage, in keeping with an elderly doctor's establishment, and the massive Sheraton sideboard had once accommodated an army of chafing dishes. For convenience, he and Vince sat together, easing Mrs Brook's serving arrangements and also the discomfort of being isolated at either end of a very long and exceedingly well-polished table intended to seat members of the large family Faro knew he was unlikely now to produce.

Mrs Brook stood by the sideboard, waiting impatiently to serve Scotch broth and a saddle of roast lamb.

Faro's hunger pangs suddenly vanished at the sight of food in such large quantities. 'We should have invited Miss Hymes to dine with us.'

'In that case she would never have boarded the Glasgow train. Besides, I fancy that she is also well beyond consuming solid food. The journey must have cost her dearly, Stepfather. As a matter of fact, I suspect that she sealed her own death warrant.'

While Vince ate his second helping of rice pudding with boyish relish and delight, and Mrs Brook closed the shutters against the dangerous vapours of the night, Faro told Vince the purpose of Maureen Hymes's visit – a sorry tale that was quite at odds with this peaceful domestic setting, enhanced by candlelight whose flickering light in the mantelpiece mirror gave shimmering life to the landscapes in their gilt-framed oil paintings. A bowl of red roses added their sweet perfume to wax polish and cracking logs.

'So, Stepfather, what are you going to do?'

Faro swore under his breath, suddenly resentful of being thrust into a situation he felt was growing rapidly out of his control. It was upon such occasions that he paused to wonder what God-forsaken destiny had led him to the Edinburgh City Police instead of a farmer's life in Orkney, which his mother would have dearly loved.

He shook his head. 'I don't know, but sometimes I think I chose the wrong job. Or maybe I'm just getting too old for it.'

Vince smiled. 'Now, Stepfather, that's not like you. You're just tired. Tomorrow and a good night's rest, and everything will look quite different. Believe me.'

CHAPTER FOUR

Two days later a letter addressed to 'Inspector Faro' arrived from Glasgow. It said briefly that Maureen Hymes had died that same night she returned from Edinburgh. 'Her last words were for you. "Tell the Inspector to remember his promise."'

Faro thrust it across the breakfast table. 'Seems you were right in your diagnosis, lad.'

'Poor creature,' said Vince as he read. 'You know, it often happens like that with twins, particularly identical more than fraternal ones. Curiously, their life-span is the same, and when one dies the other does not long survive.' Handing the letter back, he said, 'Well, Stepfather, what are you going to do now?'

'I don't see what I can do.'

Vince smiled. 'Come now, a promise is a promise, Stepfather.'

'The poor woman is dead.'

Vince shook his head. 'That is beside the point. Where, may I ask, is your chivalry?'

'Killed stone dead by twenty years with the police, I expect.' Faro sighed. 'You do talk nonsense sometimes, lad. Can you imagine me persuading the Superintendent that I want to reopen the Hymes murder case – on the dying wish of his sister?'

Vince pushed aside his breakfast egg before replying. 'Has the thought not struck you that there might be some

42

other clue that wasn't followed up in the evidence? After all, they did miss Ferris's photograph when you were off the case. Shall we have a shot at it, Stepfather?'

'We?'

'Of course.' Vince took a piece of toast and buttered it thoughtfully. 'Of course. I intend to lend a hand whenever available on the assumption – begging your pardon – that two heads are better than one. With my still somewhat scanty medical knowledge and your powers of deduction, I think we might make the perfect team. You know, Stepfather, I've always had a fancy to play policeman.' He grinned. 'Frankly, I didn't care for you when you came courting Mama— '

'I did notice,' said Faro.

Vince nodded. 'Actually, it was my secret pride at having a policeman in our family that completely converted me to having you as stepfather. How I bragged to everyone at school!'

Faro smiled. 'I'm glad there was something to redeem me in your eyes. You were far from the easiest of children.'

'I was an absolute horror,' Vince admitted cheerfully. 'So – you will let me help. Between us, we might even produce a second murderer, and wouldn't that make your policemen jolly uncomfortable!'

'I shouldn't entertain too many hopes there, lad. If he existed, and if he's wise, he will have disappeared long since. The trail is cold and whatever we find it can't help Hymes or his sister now.'

'Hymes was an idiot. You have to admit that, Stepfather.'

Faro shook his head sadly. 'You're young yet. The *crime passionnel* is the most brutal of murders to our civilised minds, the one we are least likely to excuse or forgive, of love gone sour. It is also the most frequent in the annals of crime. You haven't any idea yet what savagery can arouse even the most timid of husbands when he feels that he has been betrayed by the wife he loves.'

'Nor have I any intention of finding out. Marriage is not for ambitious young doctors with an eye to becoming Queen's Physician one day.'

'You might well do both, given time, and the right woman.'

'The right woman, Stepfather? I doubt if any such creature exists except between the covers of romantic novelettes – certainly not between wedded bedcovers, at any rate.'

When Faro smiled wryly, Vince continued, 'I see you don't believe me, but I mean it, Stepfather. As for Hymes, can you credit any man being fool enough to be hanged because of his conscience – and all for a worthless whore? He could have taken ship from Leith and been a hundred miles away. Now, the clever murderer, who uses his head and not his heart, and plans the perfect crime, I'd have respect for such a man – respect and admiration, too.'

'There's no such thing as a clever murderer, lad. They always give themselves away in the end.'

'That I don't believe. The police can be absurdly simple – not all detectives are as clever or infallible as my respected stepfather.'

'I'm far from infallible. In every eye there is a blind spot.'

'But not in yours.'

'Oh yes, in mine too.'

'Perhaps you'll meet him some day, then, this murderer who is clever enough to find your blind spot.'

'If he exists, then I hope that neither of us ever have that misfortune.'

Vince smiled. 'Come now, Stepfather, could you resist such a challenge? A man who pits his wits against all the odds, in a tricky game of life – to the death,' he added dramatically, slashing the air with an imaginary sabre.

Faro regarded him doubtfully. With all the reckless enthusiasm of youth, Vince regarded the whole idea as no end of a lark.

'Splendid. You won't forget, by the way, that we have tickets for *Othello* on Wednesday. I've told Rob and Walter that it's your favourite play, and they agree with me that you need cheering up.'

Faro thanked him bleakly. *Othello* would hardly be a cheering experience. In the hands of bungling amateurs it would probably depress him unutterably, but Vince and his friends meant well.

'Has it occurred to you, Stepfather, that there is a great deal of similarity between Othello and Hymes?'

Faro gave him a sharp look. How odd that the same idea had occurred to him at that last melancholy interview.

'Othello, you must admit,' Vince continued, 'was even more stupid than Hymes. Can you imagine any man gullible as the Moor rising to illustrious heights as Shakespeare tells us? A man who would murder his lovely young Desdemona on Iago's testimony? People don't behave like that in real life. Othello would have had a shocking row with her and then all would have been tearfully revealed.'

'Leaving no tragedy for Shakespeare to write and enthral countless generations.'

'Point to you, Stepfather.' Vince laughed and, from the desk, produced paper and pen. 'Now, back to the main business. Let us see. Are there any parallels between the murders of Mrs Hymes and Lily Goldie that might offer us some clues, besides both being employed at the convent?'

Faro considered for a moment. 'They were both young and pretty. They were even somewhat similar in appearance.'

'Indeed, the same physical types.'

'What else do we know?'

'From the post-mortem, that neither had been sexually assaulted,' said Vince. 'And Lily Goldie was not virgo intacta, but she had never borne a child.'

'We know that Sarah Hymes had run away from her husband. He suspected her of infidelity, which was not proven, except on hearsay.'

'A flirt who enjoyed teasing men and getting as much as she could from her admirers, at the same time giving as little as possible. What do we know about Goldie?'

'From your description of her at Duddingston Loch and her behaviour with the unfortunate Tim Ferris, wouldn't you say there was a very strong likeness there?'

'Exactly. If not ladies of easy virtue, then trembling on the very threshold. Goldie's background?'

'Quite respectable. An orphan, brought up by her great-aunt as companion in Galloway, which one can also interpret as an unpaid maid of all work. When the aunt, who had presumably seen that Lily was educated, died, then Lily came to Edinburgh and got a situation teaching at the convent.'

'Was it coincidence that led them both to seek employment there at the same time? In view of their flighty characters, a convent does seem a remarkable choice.'

'It isn't much to go on, but I think we might begin by calling upon the Reverend Mother, using Ferris's photograph as an excuse.' Faro looked out of the window. 'I think I'll take a walk to Greyfriars. Are you coming?'

Vince shook his head. 'No, not this time, if you don't mind. I'm going to Cramond with Rob and Walter.' He sighed and added, 'I took flowers to Mama all the time you were away . . .' He regarded Faro, sad-eyed. 'You know, I can't believe she's there – or anywhere, any more. I wish I was small again, like Rose and Emily, and could believe that dear Mama had gone to heaven and was waiting there smiling in a white robe to greet us in due course. For me, she's just – lost.'

Faro laid a sympathetic hand on his shoulder, a gesture that needed no words.

★　★　★

A grey colourless summer's day, with a high wind that turned the leaves inside out, added its melancholy to the deserted churchyard. Normally he came on Sundays, when his visit coincided with the emergence of churchgoers, but today he was glad that Vince had decided not to come. The atmosphere was oppressive, a day when it was difficult for anyone to believe that the dead were well and happy, patiently waiting in Paradise.

This was his first visit for several weeks and his path led him past a new marble stone: 'Timothy Ferris, born 1849 died 1870. Erected by his fellow students in tribute to his memory.'

That was a fine gesture for a poor lad who had no others to mourn him, Faro thought as he went on his way to that other almost new headstone which marked Lizzie's grave. Against a sombre background of urns and skulls and florid emblems of mortality, it stood out white and shining and simple.

He knelt down, attending to the flowers. He was not used to being so alone. Sunday afternoons normally saw many similarly employed in this most modern part of the burial ground. He missed the black-clad figures whose sombre attire turned the bright green summer grass into an irreverent frivolity, the widows' weeds, the men with their crêpe-draped tall-hats, the children wearing armbands.

He closed his eyes for a moment, trying to conjure up a picture of Lizzie, not as he had last seen her in those terrible hours of agony before she died, but as she would most wish to be rememberd – the smiling girl he had courted, the young and happy mother playing with Rose and Emily. Bending forward, he laid his right hand on the moulded earth in the region of her heart. He prayed, and then, as always, talked to her a little.

'What shall I do, Lizzie love? How does a fellow keep a promise to a dead woman, and one he only knew for half an hour?' Only the twittering birds answered him. 'You don't know and neither do I. Your boy thinks I should do it – as a matter of honour, he says. He's a fine clever young man. You would be proud of him. And what's more, he's your image, Lizzie love, growing more and more like you every day. And that's a great comfort to me.'

Dusting his knees, he kissed his fingers and laid them against her name so coldly upon the stone. Beset by a feeling of loneliness almost too great to be borne, he hurried back down the path, head down, jostled by the brisk wind.

Suddenly his attention was drawn to the grave of Tim Ferris, where a woman clad in grey, her face hidden in voluminous veils, stood alone. He saw that she wept. The wind fluttered a handkerchief, seized upon the swirling folds of her cape. The next moment she clutched her bonnet with its veils as both were swept from her hair to become entangled high in the shrubbery behind.

Gallantly, Faro dashed to her assistance and a delicate violet perfume assailed him. No sooner had he reached her side than her own fierce struggles released her. There was a final rending of cloth, and a moment later hat and veils were being firmly re-anchored.

But not before Faro had glimpsed a face of haunting beauty. He knew that he had met few truly beautiful women in his life. Now he and this stranger looked into each other's faces for a split second of time; the next instant, she turned away. He hovered still. Was he dismissed without one word of thanks? Sadly, that was the case. But there was more. He recognised the gesture as oddly furtive too. She did not wish to be recognised or remembered.

Turning on his heel, he walked away from that back so rigidly turned from him. He was a man in a dream, his heart thudding against his ribs, with a picture of red-gold curls, eyes of cerulean blue and a warmly seductive mouth sketched indelibly on his mind. Afterwards, trying to describe her to Vince, he could find no adequate words beyond: 'Beautiful – exquisite.'

'Young or old?' was the practical response.

'Neither. I mean, she could have been any age.'

'Could she have been one of Tim's lady-friends?'

'Perhaps.'

Vince sighed. 'You aren't a great deal of help, Stepfather. Where are all those remarkable powers of observation.'

'Blown to the four winds, I'm afraid.'

'And taken your wits with them, if I might say so. Why, you're positively besotted. Exit bereaved husband, enter lovesick swain,' he added cynically.

'That is hardly fair, Vince. I don't suppose I shall ever see her again— '

'I certainly hope not, if that was her effect upon you. How long did you say you stared at her?'

'Seconds only – a mere tantalising glimpse. But to use one of your modern terms, she was an absolute stunner.'

'Well, there's another little mystery for us. What a pity we have no excuse for including this lovely lady in our investigations. I don't suppose you'll ever find out who she was, unless you're prepared to spend a considerable time in Greyfriars Kirkyard.'

'It stands to reason that she must return to her unhappy vigil,' said Faro firmly. 'I shall go back next week at the same time, try and strike up an acquaintance.'

Vince's heavenward glance clearly indicated what he thought of his stepfather's infatuation.

The mysterious woman haunted Faro's dreams. He pursued her through the kirkyard, but when he seized her veil it was poor dying Maureen Hymes who clung to him, weeping, murmuring over and over, 'Promise . . . promise . . .' Even as he supported her, the flesh melted from her skull and he found himself holding his dead wife. 'You wept, begging me not to die. Begging me to return to you. Now you have your wish.' The nightmare continued with

Faro's bizarre reasoning as to how he was to reintroduce the decaying corpse of his dead wife to Mrs Brook and, worst of all, wondering if her son would notice how his mother had changed.

Mercifully he awoke at that moment of horror. He was sweating, he felt sick and ill as he had done so long ago in Orkney when he knew that he had seen beyond the veil of death. His grandmother had been recovered from the sea at Orkney, by repute a 'seal' woman, and his own family were endowed – or perhaps the better word was tainted – with that unhappy gift of second sight she had brought them. The dreadful nightmare from Greyfriars could neither be dismissed nor forgotten. It belonged to that unearthly no-time between sleeping and waking. And it could only be interpreted as a warning.

But of what?

CHAPTER FIVE

The Convent of the Sisters of St Anthony belonged to an earlier age than the newly sprouting villas on Edinburgh's undeveloped south side. As the sixteenth-century Babington House it had enjoyed notoriety. Belonging to a scion of the Catholic family whose ill-fated plot for the escape of Mary, Queen of Scots had cost Anthony Babington a cruel death and had signed the death warrant of his queen, the Scottish Babingtons had managed to keep clear of the scandal. They had remained staunchly but secretly Catholic and had served the Stuart cause as best they could as secret agents, while managing to avoid any public declaration which would have meant sequestration after the Forty-five.

When the last member of the family, an elderly spinster, died in the early years of the century, the house and its park was willed to the Roman Catholic Church for use as a religious house. The Sisters of St Anthony were a teaching Order, their school financed by selling the parkland as highly coveted building lots.

The ancient house had been, as Faro put it, 'somewhat freely restored', with Queen Anne and Georgian wings added to the original tower. They entered by the modern extension, bristling with turrets and gargoyles on the outside and dark panelling and marble on the inside.

A lapsed Presbyterian and non-churchgoer, Faro found embarrassing such evidence of papacy as was exhibited by religious statues and a marble fresco of the Stations of the

51

Cross. The faint smell of incense assailed their nostrils not unpleasantly, as they waited in the hall outside the newly built chapel.

The Reverend Mother's quick steps were almost inaudible on the marble floor as she came towards them, and over her normally immobile countenance flickered a look of distaste as she recognised the Inspector. She chose to ignore Vince's smile and proffered hand as Faro introduced them.

'Follow me.' In the tiny, sparsely furnished ante-room, she did not invite them to sit down. Faro's immediate reaction was that their impromptu visit was an intrusion and that his presence, and what it implied, had upset her.

'We were hoping that you might be able to help us.'

'In what way?' she asked coldly.

'In regard to Lily Goldie.'

'I see,' she said, in the tones of one who clearly did not. 'Perhaps I should point out that it is in the best interests of our girls that their normal routine is not interrupted. I need hardly tell you, Inspector, that they were all very upset – as were the sisters.' A note of annoyance shattered that calm face, pale as the wimple she wore. 'Our pupils' work and our own meditations have been seriously affected by these disruptions. May one ask what you can hope to gain from these enquiries, since the unfortunate man has paid his debt to society?'

'If you would allow me to explain. We have no intention of publicly reopening the case. This is merely a routine enquiry following your letter and the discovery of the photograph in Miss Goldie's room. I wish to check certain facts – that is all. You may rely on my discretion to disturb your establishment as little as possible.'

'Am I then to understand that you are acting in a private capacity?'

'Entirely.'

'I see.' The bloodless hands took on a supplicant's role, fingertips pressed together. 'Very well. I will do what I can to help you.'

'Were both girls of your faith?'

She looked at Vince coldly as if aware of his presence for the first time. 'Naturally. We do not knowingly take heretics into our establishment. We employ only good Catholic girls.'

'Am I correct in understanding that, though both were engaged at the same time, they were strangers to each other?' asked Faro.

The Reverend Mother shrugged. 'There was no evidence of previous acquaintance. Besides, it is extremely unlikely since they were from completely different backgrounds; one a servant, one a teacher.'

'I only asked because it did occur to me there might be some kinship.'

'Kinship?'

'Yes, they looked alike.'

'A coincidence.' She thought for a moment. 'Interesting that you should mention it though. I had on occasion mistaken each for the other – in outdoor dress that is – and out of uniform.'

Vince's triumphant glance at his stepfather said: There you are.

'May I ask you something personal?' said Faro.

The Reverend Mother hesitated for a moment. 'If it's something I can answer, then I will.'

'What were your own feelings about these murders? I'm not sure what I'm looking for,' he added frankly.

'I think I know.' She smiled thinly. 'Even nuns, Inspector, are not free from occasional flashes of what you might be tempted to call a woman's intuition. I'm afraid most of such feelings in my case relate to spiritual matters. Sarah Hymes was reluctant to go to Mass – now I understand the reason, since she had tainted her immortal soul with adultery and

53

a tissue of lies. Lily, on the other hand, I felt was not what she pretended to be, by no means a good docile Catholic girl. I felt instinctively that she had not been reared true to the faith. I can almost,' she added, with a delicate shudder, and a veiled glance at the Inspector and Vince, 'detect in the air the presence of non-Catholics. And Lily seemed to be totally ignorant of many basic matters of our religion, which made me suspect she had lied in order to obtain the situation.'

Somewhere outside a bell tolled and the Reverend Mother rose to her feet. 'I cannot help you any further and I am relying on your discretion when you make your enquiries, Inspector. Our school has suffered considerably in prospective pupils since this unfortunate scandal. I have learned one thing, and that is in future never to recruit any staff, either servants or teachers, from outside. Bear this in mind, Inspector, if you feel obliged to speak again to Sister Theresa, who found the photograph.'

There was a tap on the door, and with obvious impatience the Reverend Mother opened it. A whispered conversation. 'A moment, if you please.'

As the door closed, Vince said, 'Bless me if I can see any reason why the two women were Catholic or non-Catholic, or lied about it, should have any bearing on the case.'

'It might seem a good reason for the Reverend Mother, perhaps easier for her to understand than the *crime passionnel.*'

'I say, Stepfather, do you think we should be looking for a mad priest or a fanatical nun?' he whispered as the Reverend Mother re-entered.

Faro said, 'I should like to speak to the other teachers who were not of your Order.'

The Reverend Mother eyed him balefully as he consulted his notes. 'There were only two, besides Miss Goldie. Miss McDermot – and Miss Burnleigh, whom you interviewed during the Hymes investigations.'

'Correct.'

'As I remember, Miss Burnleigh was as baffled and shocked as the rest of us.'

'True, she couldn't help much then, but perhaps she might remember something about Miss Goldie. And I'd like to speak to Miss McDermot.'

'Then I'm afraid you are too late, Inspector.'

'Too late?'

'They are no longer with us. Miss McDermot left several weeks before the . . . er . . . first incident. She was intending to emigrate to Canada with her parents and she may have already left the country.'

'And Miss Burnleigh?'

The Reverend Mother's sigh indicated that she was becoming exasperated. 'She left us the day of the murder, I'm afraid. She had word that her mother was taken seriously ill and her presence was urgently required at home.'

'Perhaps you have her home address?'

The Reverend Mother gave him a look of ill-concealed disapproval as she unlocked a drawer in the desk. 'I have the addresses of both Miss McDermot and Miss Burnleigh.'

Faro held out his hand. 'If you please. You have been most helpful. And now, might I see Sister Theresa, if you have no objections?'

'I have made myself clear on the subject of objections, Inspector, and you must please yourself and attend the dictates of your conscience.' Accompanying them to the door, she said, 'Tell me, Inspector, how is Constable McQuinn?'

Faro remembered his first visit, how the young and very presentable constable had been greeted like an old friend by the sisters. McQuinn was well known to them and to St Anthony's, their orphan lad who had made good, and who had 'by some manner of chance' (his own vague description) come to join the Edinburgh Police Force two years earlier.

'A splendid young man,' said the Reverend Mother, and actually beamed at the Inspector, who thought sourly that McQuinn was just the kind of young man to ingratiate himself with nuns, or any other female between eighteen and eighty. Efficient and smooth, Faro should have considered him admirable. Was his unaccountable dislike based quite irrationally on a smile that was a shade too eager and a grin just a wee bit wolfish?

In the corridor, the Reverend Mother waved a hand towards the little formal garden with its arches and flower-beds and rambling roses. 'We have Danny McQuinn to thank for that. This dates from long before his police days, when he was a mere boy. He had a natural way with plants and herbs. If you would care to look around the garden, you will find that he had a hand in most of it. A very gifted boy, Inspector,' she added sternly as if reading his thoughts on the subject of McQuinn.

As they turned to leave, she said, 'A moment, Inspector. There is one question you have not asked, but one that I am quite prepared to answer.'

'And what would that be?'

'One that might or might not help. We talked earlier about woman's intuition, did we not?'

'We did.'

'Then I would be quite prepared to swear on the Holy Book that Hymes was not guilty of Lily Goldie's murder.'

'For what reason?' demanded Faro sharply.

She shook her head. 'Nothing I can lay my finger on, nothing that would be accepted in a court of law, except . . .'

'Except?'

She made a dismissive gesture with her hand. 'Except that it is all wrong somehow. Hymes was a devout Catholic, he knew all too well the consequences of endangering his immortal soul. That is precisely why he gave himself up for the murder of Sarah. Had he also murdered Lily

56

Goldie, there is not the slightest doubt in my mind that, far from denying it, he would have been most eager to make his confession and receive absolution on both accounts. After all, he had nothing to lose, his life was forfeit anyway.'

Faro and Vince exchanged glances, since this theory coincided remarkably with their own, even leaving out Hymes's religious convictions.

'There is,' continued the Reverend Mother, 'only one way it could have happened. And that is, if Lily's had been the first murder, instead of the second.'

'Murdered by mistake, you mean?'

'Yes, if in the dusk Hymes had mistaken Lily for Sarah, as I sometimes did,' she added, putting out a hand to the bell on her desk.

Sister Theresa remembered the Inspector and greeted Vince with a smile. She was stout and jolly, a *religieuse* of the Friar Tuck school, thought Faro. In complete contrast to the Reverend Mother, she was eager for a gossip about the 'unfortunate happenings' as she led the way to the room once occupied by Lily Goldie.

'This is where we found the photograph, Inspector. It had fallen from the mantelpiece here, and slipped down this loose skirting-board.'

As they were leaving, a marmalade cat sidled round the door and, finding the sister's ankles made inaccessible by her long gown, transferred his ingratiating activities to the tall Inspector.

Faro stroked the sleek coat. 'Hello, young fellow. What's your name?'

'That's Brutus — poor Brutus, we might call him now,' said Sister Theresa with a sigh. 'He belonged to Miss Goldie. Pets aren't strictly allowed by Reverend Mother, but we had a plague of mice — it's all this new building around us brings them in, I'm afraid. And Miss Goldie got him for us from Solomon's Tower.'

'Solomon's Tower? You mean the old gentleman gave the cat to her?'

'Oh, yes. She was on very friendly terms with him.'

As they followed her directions to the kitchen, Vince said, 'That was an interesting piece of information about the Mad Bart, don't you think? "Very friendly terms." Now that might be significant.'

Bet and Tina were to be found, red of face and forearms, washing sheets in the laundry. They were eager, even gleeful, at this excuse to leave their labours to talk to the Inspector, especially when he was accompanied by a handsome young gentleman. Their remarks about Lily Goldie were punctuated by coy giggles in Vince's direction. Yes, they recognised the photograph of Ferris as a sweetheart of Miss Goldie's.

'Treated him something cruel, she did.'

'That's why he fell under the train, poor soul.'

'Did Miss Goldie have any other – sweethearts – that you knew about?'

Heads were shaken. 'No.'

'There was yon wee laddie from the school at St Leonard's,' said Tina with a giggle. 'Used to skulk about waiting for her, out there by the gate.'

'You can't count him,' said Bet indignantly. 'He was no more than fourteen or fifteen.'

'What made you think he was a schoolboy then?' asked Faro.

'He was too well dressed to be an errand lad.'

'Aye, too well fed.'

'What exactly did he look like?'

'Never saw him close to. Always wore one of those big caps the school laddies wear.'

'Remember how he kept on coming to the gate, waiting for her, for days after . . .?' said Tina with a shudder.

Bet sighed. 'Aye, the poor laddie.'

'As if he couldn't believe that she wasn't coming back.'

Faro thanked them for their help and they looked yearningly at Vince, who gave them a gracious bow, which brought about more giggles.

'If you're going back to the station,' said Tina, the bolder of the two, 'remember us to Danny.'

'Danny? Oh, Constable McQuinn.'

'He used to do the gardens here before he joined the police.'

'Danny was very upset about Miss Goldie. She was always his favourite.'

'Quite sweet on her, he was,' said Tina spitefully.

'He liked all of us,' cried Bet, suddenly remembering Christian charity. 'A nice lad is Danny.'

'For a policeman,' added Tina doubtfully.

Vince's wry look in Faro's direction indicated that McQuinn had obviously ingratiated himself with an entire convent. No mean feat for a mere male, who was also a policeman.

Their road home took them past Salisbury Crags, the scene of both crimes. Aflame with the yellow gorse of summer, it was devoid long since of anything that might provide a clue.

'What about the well-dressed school laddie?' asked Vince.

'Some poor wretch that took a fancy to an older woman.'

'Thing it's worth a visit to St Leonard's School.'

'I do not,' Faro laughed. 'First a convent and then a boys' school. Bring in the whole wide world,' he sighed. 'Can you imagine how the pupils would react to a policeman's visit, or my Superintendent when he found out? Think of the fear and trembling in every heart, remembering stolen apples and other minor misdemeanours. You wouldn't get any one of them admitting to hanging about near the convent, although I dare say it happens regularly.'

'The fascination of the forbidden?'

'Exactly. Lily Goldie must have been a remarkable woman.'

'She was, Stepfather. Even on my small acquaintance with the lady, I'd say she appealed to all ages and conditions of men,' said Vince, poking at the gorse with a stick as if the answer might lie hidden there. Then he pointed dramatically towards Solomon's Tower, grey and ancient far below them. 'And what about the Mad Bart? Do you think he might be included in our list of suspects?'

Faro laughed. 'As a possible murderer, you mean? You're not serious, surely.'

Sir Hedley Marsh, known to locals as the Mad Bart, was the scion of a noble family who, according to legend, had abandoned society after some family scandal, and now lived a hermit-like existence.

'You'll have to do better than that, lad. A harmless old eccentric with a life devoted to cats.'

'But think of the opportunity. She did visit him. Surely that was in your file?'

'It was not. Another of McQuinn's curious omissions,' he said shortly. 'There was no mention of the school laddie, either.'

Vince laughed. 'Surely you wouldn't consider that a serious piece of evidence?'

'Nothing is too trivial to be included. And it's often the most innocent-seeming incidents that lead to a conviction.' He shrugged. 'I'd be more anxious to interview our infatuated school laddie, however, if his visits had ceased at the time of Goldie's murder rather than several days afterwards. Obviously, he didn't know she was dead.' Frowning, he looked towards Solomon's Tower. 'It was remarkably slipshod of McQuinn not to include a visit to our Mad Bart as a matter of routine.'

'Maybe he was misled by the harmless devotion to cats. Seriously, though, consider the proximity to both the convent and the Crags here. Don't you think—?'

'That we would be wasting our time. It's no good, Vince lad, I sometimes get the feeling that Lily Goldie is going to remain a mystery unsolved and that we'll have to settle for Hymes after all . . .'

'What? I can't believe my ears – give up so soon?' was the indignant response.

Faro sighed wearily. 'Well, we might as well see the teachers. This Miss McDermot.' He looked at the addresses. 'She's in Corstorphine. Miss Burnleigh's in Fairmilehead.'

'I'll take Corstorphine, Stepfather. One of my colleagues lives out there and he has been asking me to dine and visit the old church. That's capital. I can combine both activities.'

As he waited for dinner that evening, Faro had another look at the statements from the sisters. Brief indeed, they all expressed shock and bewilderment at the monstrous crimes, at this invasion of the cloister with violence from a world they had long since relinquished. But their overall opinions never wavered: 'Miss Goldie seemed such a nice, well-behaved young lady. Not the kind who would get herself murdered.'

But get herself murdered she had. And Faro had an instinctive feeling that it would serve no useful purpose interviewing all the inmates of the convent a second time. There was little hope of the nuns producing any new clues to Lily's possible life outside the convent walls, and he wished to steer clear of the Reverend Mother's wrath.

He sighed. Only in a convent could two women have lived for months and made so little impression. Obviously religious ladies also gave up the natural curiosity associated with their sex, along with other worldly pleasures, when they took their final vows.

And for once, realising the magnitude of his self-appointed task, he understood why his colleagues had been so anxious to settle for Hymes as a double-murderer.

About the teachers they had still to interview, he felt more hopeful. People suffering from shock have unreliable memories, and some fact or observation forgotten about, or dismissed as too trivial, when they were first questioned might, in retrospect, assume more significant proportions.

He would begin by hiring a gig tomorrow and driving out to Fairmilehead village to see Miss Burnleigh. But tonight . . .

'Tonight we have the Pleasance Theatre, Stepfather. Shakespeare will be a capital opportunity for you to relax. A nice murder, on stage for a change, that you can watch and enjoy, without having to solve.'

CHAPTER SIX

The Pleasance Theatre was already crowded and the curtain about to rise on *Othello* when Faro and Vince arrived. Vince had been delayed by Dr Kellar and Faro secretly hoped they might not be expected to go after all, if the performance had already begun.

To his annoyance, he found his stepson in no way perturbed and quite ready to sacrifice his dinner, much to Mrs Brook's indignation.

'Put it in the oven, indeed. What sort of way is that for a young doctor to treat his stomach, or my rib of roast lamb?'

They arrived breathless, and Vince seized the only seats available in the back row. 'Rob and Walter won't be allowed to keep seats for us as late as this, I'm afraid. That would create ill-feeling, not to say a riot, among the other students who have waited for hours.' As the curtain rose, he added, 'They must be down near the front, dammit. Can you see at all?'

'Good job I'm tall.'

Vince grinned. 'At least we can stand up with no one behind us. Sorry, Stepfather. It's all my fault.'

Faro was non-committal, irritated at having been pressed to attend the play and then finding himself in a poor seat. However, he reflected by the end of the first scene, there were some advantages, and if Mr Topaz Trelawney's Thespians hadn't given a better account of themselves by

63

the time the curtain fell at the end of Act I, he would make some excuse and slip out. Vince would not mind; he had his two friends to meet in the green-room for refreshments.

As cat-calls and loud applause from the noisy audience greeted Othello's first appearance, Faro groaned. It seemed that all his fears had been justified. Mr Topaz Trelawney was an actor-manager, a Shakespearean tragedian of the worst kind. He over-acted, leering, gesturing, making asides to the audience, which delighted them but turned Othello into a buffoon. An inch deep in greasepaint, his overweight frame filled the tawdry costume to overflowing as he pranced and strutted across the stage. Rather too often for comfort, he forgot his lines and took a reassuring swig from a tankard placed on a convenient table. These forays, which grew more frequent as the play progressed, affected his posturing with an alarming unsteadiness.

Faro stirred restlessly in his seat. The performance was exactly what he had expected. It was unendurable, and he would leave at the end of Act I. Scene 2 dragged wearily to a close, and as Desdemona's entrance had been well signalled, Faro groaned, expecting the worst. Then, in Scene 3, thunderous applause greeted her first appearance.

A flower-like Desdemona, with long flowing blonde hair, a voice of astonishing beauty and timbre, which she had no need to raise for it carried with a pure, bell-like quality to the back row of the theatre. While she spoke, she held her audience captive and it was as if no one else existed on stage. Her presence turned Iago, Cassio, Emilia – and particularly Othello – into stiff cardboard painted characters.

The audience loved her, they hung upon every word of her three short speeches, her duty to her father Brabantio and to her husband Othello and her plea to accompany him. As Faro too now waited enthralled, trying to remember the

64

play and when she would appear again, he lost all interest in going home. He forgot the discomfort of his seat, the atrocious over-acting of the Thespians, for he recognised that he was in the presence of that exceedingly rare creature, a great natural actress, who could convey without raising her voice, without outrageous posturing or gestures, a child-like innocence, her love and hero-worship of Othello and a desperate vulnerability.

The curtain fell at the end of Act II, and watching his stepfather applaud, Vince added his 'Bravos' to those of the student audience. As they joined the noisy good-natured throng heading for the green-room, where refreshments were served in the interval, Vince said:

'Isn't Alison Aird an absolute wonder? Can't you see why we're all passionately in love with her? Desdemona's just a small role. Wait until you see Alison Aird as Lady Macbeth or Cleopatra.'

Vince's two companions, Rob and Walter, emerged through the crowd, and Faro, who had found a small table, set pints of ale before them.

'Guess what, Stepfather. Walter's cousin Hugo Rich is playing Cassio – joined the company two months ago. This is his first major role and we've been cordially invited to a party back-stage. You'll come with us, of course.'

Normally Faro would have resisted meeting the Trelawney Thespians, but if Desdemona in her real-life role as Mrs Trelawney would be there he felt this was an opportunity not to be missed.

Desdemona's handkerchief scene and Othello's brutality brought storms of protest from the audience, especially as the latter's performance grew more and more outrageous and considerably less steady. Faro spared a thought for that inebriated gentleman, doubtless seeking consolation in the bottle for the fact that he was a dismal failure as an actor. How many performances would it take for Trelawney to recognise that his own future as well as that of his

Thespians hung on a slender thread – that the audience came to applaud Mrs Aird, and that the success of every evening belonged to his leading lady.

How Trelawney must hate all that adulation by-passing him each night. Faro tried to picture them as man and wife in a cosy domestic setting, but imagination baulked.

The Willow Song in Act IV was a triumph of under-statement, made all the more moving. The audience was spellbound now and Faro decided that this lovely woman must indeed be bound to the Thespians by ties of loyalty and love, when her talents so obviously belonged in the ranks of the great Shakespearean actors on the stages of London and New York.

'Kill me tomorrow: let me live tonight.' The words, uttered in no more than a whisper, reached every seat in the house, and sent a chill through Faro. For a moment he forgot that this was a play he was watching. Helpless to avert the tragedy, he expected to see Desdemona's lifeless form in Othello's arms.

And at the last, 'Commend me to my kind lord', the silence was broken by an outburst of scuffling as many of the audience began to take their departure before the curtain fell. It also released Faro from his spell. What was coming over him? he wondered. That strange dark moment out-of-time on stage – too many wife-slayers?

He joined the tumultuous applause as the curtain rose on a smiling Desdemona, risen unscathed from her death-bed. She very obviously supported Othello to his curtain-speech, which was clearly not as reverently received as Mr Topaz Trelawney thought proper to the occasion. He made a drunken, threatening gesture to the audience, quickly suppressed by an anxious Desdemona, and the curtain mercifully descended.

The audience surged towards the exits, while Faro and Vince made their way back-stage to the small dressing-room Hugo Rich shared with the other male members of the cast. Topaz Trelawney, Faro noticed, had a room of his own.

Hugo greeted them anxiously. 'How did it look from the front?'

Walter was full of assurances; Rob and Vince were kind and flattering about his Cassio, putting him at his ease. Mark their words, they would be seeing him treading the boards of the London stage one day very soon. He went away, beaming and happy.

The party increased in volume of noise and merriment as they were joined by a troupe of girls who were part of the company. Faro, alert, looked in vain for Desdemona among these young actresses, who made costumes, attended to laundry and more mundane domestic matters when there were no suitable parts for them.

They were polite to him, and attentive, respectful and courteous in a manner that made him conscious of his age, and of the fact that he had lived and experienced a whole lifetime before any of them were born. By the time he was watching Vince with a girl sitting on his knee, he decided that his presence was superfluous and that he should quietly withdraw. Sheridan Place and his bed, only minutes away, seemed a tempting alternative.

Catching Hugo's eye, he made his apologies about work the next morning, adding, 'No, please, don't disturb Vince.'

'I will see you to the door,' said Hugo. 'Yes, I must. It is a rule that everyone is seen out and the door re-locked. There are often unsavoury characters about and once the box office was robbed.'

As they walked along the dimly lit corridor, the door next to Trelawney's opened and a girl emerged and hurried towards the exit ahead of them. She turned, smiling, to let Hugo open the door for her, and Faro found himself staring into the face of the woman he had last seen in Greyfriars Kirkyard, by the grave of Timothy Ferris.

'Goodnight, Hugo,' she said and stepped out into the darkness.

'Who was that?' he asked Hugo. 'Is she a friend of Trelawney's?'

Hugo smiled. 'I suppose you could call her that.' Then he added, with a great roar of laughter, 'Don't tell me, sir, that you don't recognise Desdemona.'

'Desdemona? But . . . but . . .'

'The long blonde hair is a wig.' And seeing the Inspector's astonished face, he said, 'I would have introduced you, but I'm afraid I didn't catch your name. Mrs Aird is in a great hurry as usual, a carriage usually awaits her each night.'

Outside, blinded by the sudden darkness, Faro became aware of the cloaked figure of Alison Aird pacing the pavement.

Raising his hat, expecting a rebuff, he said, 'Forgive this intrusion, ma'am. I should like to say how greatly I enjoyed your performance tonight. May a complete stranger be permitted to find a carriage for you?' As he spoke, he was conscious of her nervous reaction to his approach. It seemed a long time before she said:

'If you would be so good, sir. I fear some misfortune has overtaken the brougham which normally collects me after the performance.' She sighed. 'My departure was delayed tonight with business matters, hence the mix-up.'

'This should not take long. There is a hiring establishment within hailing distance. Stay close to the stage door. If you are in any difficulties, you need just ring the bell.' And Faro set off at top speed, chuckling to himself, delighted at his good fortune in finding his beauty in distress.

Luck was with him and he found a gig almost immediately. Returning with it, panic-stricken, he almost expected her to be gone.

He sighed with relief when her shadowy figure emerged from the stage door. Giving directions to a street a half-mile distant, she turned to Faro. 'You have been very kind. Perhaps I might offer you a lift?'

'I would be delighted,' said Faro, deciding the opportunity of sharing a cab was too great to miss.

Alison Aird settled herself and stared out of the window. It promised to be a silent journey.

'I was quite enthralled by the play tonight,' said Faro desperately.

In the darkness, her voice smiled. 'Why, thank you again.'

'Regrettably, I have been absent from Edinburgh and have missed most of your season here. But I do hope to see others.' Even to himself, he sounded nervous, too anxious to please.

'I trust you will also find them enjoyable,' said Alison Aird, returning her attention to the passing night, the flicker of torches from other carriages.

'How do you find Edinburgh?'

'Beautiful but lonely.'

Faro's mind again presented the melancholy picture of Alison Aird in Greyfriars. What had been her relationship to young Ferris? Were they lovers, or kin? He could see no resemblance to Ferris's photograph and had never seen the young man alive. He also realised that off-stage his Desdemona was older than appeared at first glance.

'Have you been long with the Thespians?'

'Just this season. This is my first time in Scotland for many years. But I am by birth a Scotswoman.'

'Alison Aird would imply that.'

'Indeed, it is my real name.'

'I gather you are not Mrs Topaz Trelawney.'

'Good gracious, no. Whatever gave you that idea?' She laughed. 'Mr Trelawney is merely my employer. He was once a very great actor,' she said in his defence, 'one I admired greatly.'

Faro could think of no suitable comment, beyond secret delight that his Desdemona was unmarried. 'Have you ever considered the London stage, Miss Aird?'

There was a pause before she replied, 'It is Mrs Aird. And your name, sir?'

'Faro. Jeremy Faro.'

She looked out of the window, and said, he thought with a certain relief, 'Ah, here is my destination. Thank you for escorting me, Mr Faro.' Handing her down from the carriage, he made a mental note of the house and street number before giving the driver instructions for Sheridan Place.

'The mourning lady from Greyfriars,' said Vince at breakfast next morning. 'Are you absolutely sure? After all, you only had a glimpse of her.'

'A glimpse I will never forget.'

'But what an astonishing coincidence.'

'Is she a widow?'

'No idea. Sometimes actresses use Mrs as a courtesy title. But she isn't Trelawney's wife.'

'I know. She told me so.'

'What about Tim? Did she offer any explanation?'

'There was no time to ask.'

Vince thought for a moment. 'I expect Tim was one of her many admirers. Come to think of it, we used to see him at performances.'

'Alone?'

'Yes, always alone.'

'There must have been some intimate connection, otherwise why dress up in all those ridiculous veils, so that she wouldn't be recognised visiting his grave?'

Vince smiled. 'Really, Stepfather, you are quite an innocent sometimes. The answer is obvious. They were lovers. After all, she can't be more than thirty-five. Maybe we're wrong. Maybe it's she who rejected him, not Lily Goldie.'

'The same thought has just occurred to me, lad.'

'The sense of guilt would appeal to the actress in her, and visiting his grave be a kind of performance of grief.'

'You make it sound very calculated, lad.'

Vince shrugged. 'I know actresses, Stepfather.'

'What are they doing next?'

'Macbeth. Hugo's playing Second Murderer. And Mrs Aird gives a riveting performance as Lady Macbeth.'

CHAPTER SEVEN

Urgent matters concerning a break-in at Holyrood Palace occupied Faro's immediate attention and, much as he chafed at the delays, he realised that he had taken on the case of Lily Goldie as a private investigation. In future, he could expect to devote only his spare time to it, and he was glad indeed of Vince's proposed assistance.

Later that week, with the prospect of a day off, he decided it would be opportune to make the postponed visit to Miss Burnleigh at Fairmilehead.

On his way to the gig-hiring establishment, he saw a figure emerging from the direction of Causewayside. Although she was too distant to recognise her features, his heart's sudden lurch told him this was Mrs Aird. He was quite elated when she smiled and raised her hand in greeting from across the road. He obviously hadn't been forgotten.

'It is Mr Faro, is it not?'

'You are looking well, Mrs Aird,' said Faro, bowing over her hand, wanting to say that she looked divinely adorable, her face flushed and her bonnet a little askew from the stiff breeze blowing down from Arthur's Seat.

Again she smiled at him, her manner relaxed, inviting conversation. Faro's mind had suddenly emptied of social chat and, sounding infernally dull, even to himself, he said, 'I trust your lodgings are comfortable and to your liking?'

She nodded, frowning. Did she think him tight-lipped and unfriendly? Dear God, did he have to sound so stiff and formal?

'This area is no place for a gentlewoman these days.'

'You mistake me, Mr Faro. I am no gentlewoman, just an ordinary actress— '

'But the area is insalubrious – have you not been warned of its dangers?' He pointed to the wooden palisades that divided Minto Street, where they were standing, from Causewayside. 'There is another such at Salisbury Road. What do you think they are for, Mrs Aird? They are to keep thieves and vagabonds, the wild beasts who lurk around Wormwoodhall and the Sciennes from infiltrating into a decent respectable neighbourhood. The rowdies who break the peace are, alas, the New Town puppies from this side and the keelies from Causewayside.' He stopped, breathless, not having meant to indulge in such a long speech.

'Indeed? Does that also account for the lodge gates at both ends of Sheridan Drive? To keep it select?'

Feeling uncomfortably that she was laughing at him, he replied, 'I don't know about select, but I hope you will not be tempted into this area after nightfall.'

'That is highly unlikely.' And she looked away, like someone suddenly bored, as well she might be, he thought desperately. Politely, she said, 'I will bear in mind your good advice. But I am delaying you . . .'

'Not at all. It is a pleasure to talk to you again.'

'Is it really?' There was sincere surprise in her voice and her accompanying smile which made him realise that her first impressions had been far from favourable. She doubtless thought him oafish, a pompous bore.

'I was on my way to hire a gig to go to Fairmilehead tomorrow. Over there,' he pointed, 'on the approaches to the Pentlands.'

'I've been wondering about those hills. They are very tempting, some day I mean to explore them.'

'Why not tomorrow, then? Why not come with me?' The words had burst out of him as if of their own accord as he towered over her, stammering, blushing like a schoolboy.

She put a hand to her mouth. 'Oh, I did not mean to intrude . . .'

'Of course you didn't. But as this is a purely routine matter of business, I would – would enjoy your company.'

Faro walked home, conscious that his step had lightened considerably. He chuckled delightedly, feeling that he had shed twenty years in the past ten minutes.

Mrs Brook met him with a message that Vince was to spend the night at Corstorphine. 'I was to tell you that he would attend to the business you had discussed before returning to Edinburgh.'

So Vince was to call on Miss McDermot. Good lad. And before closing his eyes that night, Faro said, 'God, I know how busy you are and I haven't asked you for anything since you decided to take Lizzie and the wee lad away from me. But, please God, if you can spare the time for this small request, please, let it be a fine day tomorrow. Keep the rain off. That's all I ask.'

His prayer was answered. He collected the gig in the radiant sunshine of early summer. Ten minutes later he was sitting outside Mrs Aird's lodging. Tucking the blanket about her, he was again assailed by that feeling of light-hearted youth. When in recent times had he felt as young as this? As they jogged down the road together, her arm comfortably close to his own, their legs touching as they took a corner, he had to restrain the longing to put an arm about her shoulders and look into that pretty face instead of staring at the road ahead.

She was a convert to the Quaker religion, she told him, and had been visiting the Meeting House at Causewayside. The actress in her brought vividly to life the characters she had met, those who remembered the area as a thriving

74

weaving community, their Edinburgh shawls sought after as far away as New York shops.

Faro was at peace at her side, content to listen, as they climbed past fields and woods and the grey clutter of villages. Then a distant prospect of the castle brooding darkly down upon the smoking chimneys of Edinburgh, justifying Robert Burns's epithet of 'Auld Reekie'.

A train crawled, puffing importantly and thinly along the railway line, and tiny ships were tacking in the Forth. Their passing gig brought forth from every farm the warning bark of dogs, the agitation of barnyard fowls. A curlew swooped, crying, and for Faro the feeling of *déjà vu* persisted. Had his companion not already said those words, laughed like that at a solemn donkey staring over a hedge, exclaimed delightedly at the sight of children feeding a lamb? He looked at her, filling the empty corners of his life with such grace and harmony, amazed anew that fate had given no warning, no allowance for this intrusion into his life.

Alison Aird was a stranger, but already as she spoke each contour of her face shaped itself into a familiar pattern. As each gesture struck a chord of remembrance, he found himself at the mercy of his own background, which he was careful to conceal from public gaze and comment. The second sight his seal-woman grandmother had bequeathed to him had never seen an occasion for rejoicing.

That intuition accounted for perhaps ten per cent of his success as a detective, and had more than once been a factor in putting him in the right direction of vital clues. It did not always work in his private life, alas. He had no warning when his sweet Lizzie bore their son that she and the boy would be dead, lost and gone for ever, in a matter of days.

'And Hugo tells me that the handsome young doctor is your stepson,' Mrs Aird was saying. Could it be that she had been enquiring about him? He was flattered.

'Indeed. I am a widower, with two little girls living up north with their grandmother. What of you – is Mrs Aird a courtesy title only?'

She shook her head and sighed. 'Would that it were so. I am a widow.' She cut short his commiserations. 'It is a long time ago, and I was married for such a short time that I have almost forgotten the experience.' Pausing, she added, 'I was not so fortunate as yourself, my only child also died.' Then, as a tactful indication that the subject was closed, she pointed a gloved hand. 'Over there. Is that our destination?'

Before them lay Fairmilehead, a huddle of roofs and smoking chimneys with two thread-like roads joining beside a wood heavy with summer trees.

'Journey's end.' He wondered, could it be the same for her? The completion of another journey they had begun together in a world whose shadowy confines were long lost to them?

He looked into her eager smiling face. How unbelievable that this feeling of familiarity was all wrong. This was but their third meeting. And he knew already, with painful certainty, that before the day was ended and they returned in the gig, his heart would be lost to her.

Faro's natural reaction was rebellion at the idea of falling in love again, with all that it entailed. Green love-sickness was the last thing a detective needed, especially a man nearly forty. He knew that his powers of detection worked more efficiently without domestic ties. That was his main reason for distancing himself from his young daughters in Orkney. Even happily married, he had known that he would be a better policeman on his own, with the kind of life he lived, with its uncertain hours, its possible dangers.

While delighting in the experience of having her by his side, he groaned inwardly, suddenly cursing himself for his own folly, wishing he had not asked her, or that she had refused to come. Damn it, how could he help this feeling of rapture? He was helpless to escape, rushing headlong into whatever torments lay ahead. He had thought with Lizzie's death that this chapter of his life had closed for ever, that nothing would again interfere with his dedication. Was he yet to discover that love was eternal, that as long as a man breathed it lurked inescapable on that road from birth to death?

'Do you wish me to wait for you here?'

'You may accompany me, if you wish.'

She frowned. 'You mentioned a business engagement – I would not wish to intrude.'

Faro smiled. 'I am a police officer, Mrs Aird – a detective. And this is a mere routine enquiry.'

Mrs Aird looked startled. 'I had no idea, sir. I presumed you were a business man of some sort. You have the look of an advocate.'

'I wish I was as affluent.' Faro smiled.

She gave him a hard look. 'I will remain here, Mr Faro, and wait for you.' She opened the large handbag she carried. 'I have a script to read – my lines, you know.'

'You are sure? I will be as quick as I can.' And tucking the rug around her, Faro started off down the road, where he stopped an old man, bent double over a stick, and asked directions to Hill Cottage, Mill Lane. 'Number fifteen, it says here.'

The answer was a shake of the head. 'There's no cottage of that name hereabouts. The general store'll mebbe know – newcomers, are they?'

'Burnleigh, did you say? Number fifteen?' repeated the woman behind the counter, with a shake of her head. 'People don't go much by numbers here. I don't know the name and my man Jock's the posty. He'd be able to tell you but he's away in the far pasture. But there's Mill Lane, you can see for yourself, across there.'

Mill Lane was old and cobbled, the cottages huddled in antiquity. The numbers ran out at eleven. Faro pondered, and took a chance on number eleven, where a young woman answered the door, obviously in the middle of feeding the crying baby in her arms. No, she had never heard of any Burnleighs. 'Look, there's Jock – see him, he'll know.'

Hurrying back along the lane, Faro once more repeated the story, this time at the top of his voice, as Jock was more than slightly deaf.

'There's no' many folk biding here and I ken them all. Besides, Burnleigh is an unusual name, I would remember a name like that.'

'I was told that she had come back from Edinburgh – she was a teacher at the convent in Newington – to take care of her mother who was ailing and had sent for her.'

Jock shook his head. 'I canna help ye, I'm sorry.'

Faro walked back towards the gig, deep in thought. Here was something odd indeed. Was this what he was waiting for? Why had Miss Burnleigh chosen to disappear at the time of Lily Goldie's murder, leaving a false address?

He felt the familiar twitch of danger alerted. Had he stumbled on a clue to the identity of the second murderer at last?

Alison Aird put away her script as he took his seat beside her in the gig. 'Were your enquiries successful?' she asked, curious as to his preoccupation.

'I am more baffled than ever,' he said, suddenly needing to tell her the real reason for his visit.

'A teacher at the convent, you said. Was that where the recent murders took place?'

'It was.'

'I thought the murderer had been hanged?'

'I thought so too . . .' And Faro went on to tell her of the visit of Maureen Hymes. 'I keep asking myself why Clara Burnleigh left a false address and spun a tissue of lies about going home to a sick mother, when neither mother nor the house exist.'

'It might not be entirely sinister, of course,' said Mrs Aird. 'It might mean only that she preferred not to tell the truth?'

'But why?'

Mrs Aird smiled. 'Well, it's perfectly easy for another woman to understand.'

'Is it indeed?'

'I can see you're a stickler for truth at all times, Inspector, but Miss Burnleigh's deception might be more readily explained.'

'In what way?'

She laughed. 'The most natural of ways. Imagine she had a lover – a married man – and she has gone off with him. She would hardly be likely to wish to confess that to the Reverend Mother. Or, far more likely, she had the offer of a better situation and was too embarrassed to tell the truth – a white lie, a piece of face-saving, so as not to hurt her employer's feelings.'

'I still think Miss Burnleigh's behaviour needs investigating.'

'Ah, but that is because you are looking at it from the point of view of crime being involved, trying to exercise your deductive powers and find a hidden criminal motive when in fact the whole thing is no more than innocent deception.'

'We're back to deception again – and I must once again disagree with you. In my book there is no such thing as innocent deception. Mrs Aird, you are talking in paradoxes.'

Mrs Aird shrugged. 'Paradoxes are all too often a necessary part of a female's survival in this man's world. It is part of our nature to be devious upon occasion.'

Faro could think of no suitable reply, and as they came in sight of the Pleasance again the sun was setting on Arthur's Seat. A tranquil evening in a world where only man – or woman, when occasion demanded, according to

Mrs Aird – was vile. Be that as it may, he was reluctant to let the evening end.

'Shall we continue into Princes Street Gardens, listen to the band for a while?'

Mrs Aird shook her head. 'Forgive me, but I must return to my lodging.'

At least she offered no excuse, no white lie, but Faro found himself wishing that she had, despite their earlier conversation. It was easier for his male pride to accept an excuse than what he must presume: that she had had enough of him and his dour society for one day. Had he thrown away, by his own folly, an excellent chance of further acquaintance? Thinking back over the day, he felt he had not acquitted himself too well. On almost every score he could have done better. Would Mrs Aird consider him worthy of another chance?

While he waited impatiently for Vince's return home that evening, he hoped that the interview with Miss McDermot had been more productive. Whatever Mrs Aird's explanations, he found the disappearance of Miss Burnleigh so near to the murder of Lily Goldie oddly sinister, and felt that somehow the two were connected.

It was late when Vince arrived home. His first question was, 'Well, Stepfather, how was Fairmilehead?'

'Another mystery, lad.'

Vince listened in silence to Faro's story of the missing Miss Burnleigh. 'Well, I hope you did better with Miss McDermot.'

'At least Miss McDermot exists, very prettily, too. I was just in time to find her emigrating to Canada.' He groaned. 'She goes on the next sailing – in two days – I'm quite heartbroken . . .'

'I accept that, but did she tell you anything useful?'

'It seems that Lily Goldie didn't care much for her fellow teachers, or for female company in general. However, she did mention that on two occasions when she was out collecting nature specimens she observed Lily leaving Solomon's Tower.'

'So? We already know that from Sister Theresa. Presumably she was negotiating the transfer of a kitten.'

'You really think that's all?'

'Look, lad, occasionally our Mad Baronet, an ardent Calvinist who hates popery, rains down biblical curses on passing inmates of St Anthony's, calling them the whores of Babylon. And he carries on a war of insults and threats with the boys at St Leonard's School.'

Vince tapped the notes on Faro's desk. 'I imagine they torment him. But he did entertain a young and attractive teacher from the convent. Could he have made some improper advance, been repelled and had a brainstorm?'

'I'll be the most surprised man on the force if you're right, lad. But thanks for all your trouble.'

'No trouble at all, Stepfather. It was a very great pleasure – although, alas, a short-lived one – to meet the delectable Miss McDermot.' He sighed.

'By the way,' said Faro, trying to sound casual, 'I took Mrs Aird with me to Fairmilehead.'

'Mrs Aird?' Vince's eyebrows shot upwards. 'How did you manage that?'

'Met her out walking when I was hiring the gig. She expressed interest in the distant view of the Pentlands and announced herself delighted to accompany me.'

'Well!' Vince was obviously impressed. 'And what did you find out about the delectable Mrs Aird?'

'That she is in fact a widow – husband long dead.'

'Anything about Tim Ferris?' When Faro shook his head, Vince said, 'It's quite possible that she didn't know of his association with Lily Goldie and believed that he had committed suicide because of her.'

'Since you suggested it, I've been thinking along those lines too. Perhaps a closer acquaintance with Mrs Aird will reveal all.'

'Have you another assignation?'

'Not immediately.' When Vince looked disappointed, his stepfather, not wishing to lose face, said hastily, 'She is very involved with her next role for the Thespians.'

'I should have thought she would have them all off by heart by now.'

Faro offered no further comment and left for the Central Office, where he found an urgent message awaiting him. A message which suggested that his forebodings had been right and that they were now dealing with the murder of a third victim.

The body of a young woman had been washed up at Cramond Island.

CHAPTER EIGHT

Faro knew the Cramond area well. He and Vince often spent a pleasant afternoon canoeing on the River Forth and taking a picnic on the island. Constable Danny McQuinn had been off-duty visiting in the area and had been the first on the scene when the alarm was raised.

'A little lad was playing at the water's edge – he made the discovery. They put up the alarm flag for the boatman, since it was high tide and they'd had to drag the body ashore in case it drifted out to sea again.'

Faro sighed. 'Thereby destroying any likely clues.'

'Clues, sir. There weren't many clues. I'd reckon this was a suicide.'

'Oh, and what reasons would you have for that conclusion?'

McQuinn thought for a moment. 'Young she was, fully clothed – at least, she had been when she fell in. Looked as if she might have been in the water for a week or two.'

'Any means of identification?'

'Not any obvious ones. It wasn't my duty to carry out an investigation. That was for the police surgeon,' he reminded Faro. 'Is that all, sir? I believe they are doing the post-mortem now.'

Faro nodded. Vince had accompanied Dr Kellar to the mortuary.

'Before you go – a moment. You didn't by any chance recognise the body, did you, as that of Miss Clara Burnleigh?'

Constable McQuinn stared at him, and then blushed furiously. 'Miss – Miss Burnleigh? You mean from the convent?'

'I mean precisely that.'

'Well ... no. I didn't know Miss Burnleigh was a missing person, sir. I understood she had returned home to take care of a sick parent.'

'She told you that?'

'Why should she? I mean, it was common knowledge in the convent.'

'But you knew her quite well?'

'I did?'

'According to the sisters, you were very friendly with the teachers, so I naturally imagined you would be able to recognise if the dead body belonged to Miss Burnleigh.'

Again a tell-tale flush rose in the region of McQuinn's neck. Faro suppressed a grim smile. What a desperate handicap in his profession. How could anyone take seriously a policeman who blushed like a schoolboy? This time it was anger.

'The body had been in the water some time. It would be very difficult for anyone to recognise her at a passing glance. And I certainly wasn't on those sort of terms with the lady and I certainly wasn't expecting it to be any other than a stranger.' Looking at his superior's stony face, he asked, 'Has something happened to Miss Burnleigh?'

'I wish I knew. I was trying to track her down, some routine enquiries about Lily Goldie's murder— '

'I understood that case was closed, Inspector.'

'It is, it is,' said Faro irritably.

'Oh, I see,' said McQuinn slowly. 'Did you try Fairmilehead?'

'I did indeed, but the address she gave doesn't exist and no one has ever heard of her mother, Mrs Burnleigh.'

'So you think she might have been murdered?'

'I certainly think there is a strong possibility. Tell me,

when you were on friendly terms, did she talk to you about her home?'

'Only that she lived at Fairmilehead and had a widowed mother,' said McQuinn guardedly.

'Well, this body that's been washed up. Was it her?' Faro demanded impatiently.

McQuinn suppressed a shudder of distaste. 'Like I told you, sir. I didn't look very hard.'

'A policeman can't afford such sensitive feelings. For heaven's sake, man, identifying corpses is all part of the routine, or didn't they tell you that when you joined up?'

'It couldn't be Clara Burnleigh, sir. Why should she want to commit suicide?' said McQuinn defiantly.

'That's what we've got to find out. And while we're on the subject, I've been looking at your interviews following Lily Goldie's murder. I find none relating to Sir Hedley Marsh, whom I am told she visited frequently.'

'Seeing that all the evidence pointed to Hymes and he had given himself up, I hardly thought it necessary to disturb the old gentleman. It would have been a mere formality.'

'In a murder enquiry, nothing is a mere formality. Remember that in future.' Faro felt his temper rising. I must watch it, control my emotions where McQuinn is concerned. Or one of these days, I am going to resort to physical violence.

Fortunately for both men, Superintendent Mackintosh came into the office at that moment.

'Well, what are you waiting for, McQuinn?' McQuinn saluted and departed gratefully.

'About this Cramond corpse, sir,' said Faro.

'Positive identification might take some time. Nothing you need concern yourself over at the moment. From Kellar's report, there's no evidence of foul play. But you'd better be ready for anything that comes up.'

Faro realised that patience would be required as the list of fifty missing females notified to the Central Office by anxious relatives was checked. Where the description tallied with the new-found corpse, the unpleasant visit to the mortuary lay ahead for those who had waited, some for days only, some for much longer, for that moment of awful revelation of whether they had at last discovered a missing daughter, sister, wife or friend.

The newspapers would also announce the discovery, and that was always calculated to bring in a fresh crop of enquiries from deserted lovers and husbands. In particular, those who had not considered that the storming out and disappearance after a quarrel was a matter worthy of police investigation. Faro felt impatient of the delays involved, sure that, if this was a murder case, time was of the essence, but he could hardly explain his feelings to Superintendent Mackintosh, who would take a very dim view of one of his detectives carrying out a private investigation into a murder that was officially closed.

As he was leaving the office, the Superintendent called him in. 'There's a ship docking at Leith on the evening tide. And we've been tipped off that there's contraband aboard. This is maybe what we've been waiting for. See to it, will you, Faro.'

The warning had come too late. Faro spent a chilly evening in Leith investigating the ship's papers, talking to her captain while policemen and Excise officers carefully checked over the cargo and every possible hiding place in the ship.

Returning home, Faro realised that in the Pleasance Theatre the curtain had now risen on Alison Aird as Lady Macbeth. Disgruntled and weary, he sat down at his desk and carefully re-read his notes and his new information on Lily Goldie.

As he did so, he realised grimly that if the body at Cramond proved to be Clara Burnleigh, they were in all probability dealing with a multi-murderer, who might even now be stalking his fourth victim.

In the interval, he decided on a further visit to the Reverend Mother at St Anthony's. A daunting prospect, for he would not be welcome, but he was certain that she had the strength, needed in her calling, not to shrink from what she considered her duty, no matter how distressing or distasteful the task – and even if it meant visiting the mortuary and identifying the corpse as that of Miss Burnleigh.

That was tomorrow. Tonight, he felt the stage in his investigations had been reached where he needed to consult his notes, and with his own observations and conclusions draw up a comprehensive account of the suspects and clues to date.

In his neat, precise handwriting, Faro headed the document:

The Convent Murders: Evidence and Clues thus far

1. Post-Mortem Evidence. Neither Hymes nor Goldie, who had described themselves for the convent records as 'spinster' when examined were found to be virgins. (In the case of Hymes only, there was evidence of child-bearing, and she had indeed borne two children.) Although their deaths had been violent, neither woman had been sexually assaulted.

2. Both the Mother Superior of St Anthony's and Hymes's twin sister Maureen had presented very valid arguments against Patrick Hymes having been the murderer of Lily Goldie. According to the Reverend Mother, he was a devout Catholic and remained so to the end, he would have confessed and wished to receive the Church's absolution for, both murders. This testimony had been confirmed by Maureen Hymes, who stated that her brother, this apparently ignorant, ill-educated member of the Irish labouring class, had once been destined for the priesthood.

3. According to the Reverend Mother, the two murdered women were physically similar. Hymes could more likely have been guilty had Goldie been his first victim – that is, if he had mistaken her for his wife in semi-darkness and sprung upon her in murderous rage. This theory does not make sense with Goldie the second victim, especially as by then Hymes had already settled accounts with his erring wife.

4. The two women, servant and teacher, were employed at the convent and arrived about the same time. Was this fact significant when allied to their physical similarity and dubious morals? Could it have some bearing on the subsequent events? Could Goldie's murderer have been a fanatical inmate, a nun, outraged by such behaviour?

5. The Mad Baronet. Were Goldie's visits as innocent as they seemed? Worth investigating.

6. Would an infatuated schoolboy who hung about watching for Goldie be able to throw any light on her last hours, always presuming that he could be tracked down at St Leonard's?

7. Clara Burnleigh. Did the fact that she had given a false address, and was probably using a false name, have some bearing on Goldie's murder? Is she still alive or is she the third victim at present lying in the mortuary? If so, then we are dealing with a serious wave of murders, and we can expect more of them until the assassin is apprehended.

After some thought, Faro added another name:

8. Danny McQuinn. He had an intimate knowledge of the convent, had access as a respected protégé of the Reverend Mother, and was a former gardener and odd-job man. According to the two maids, he was

'sweet' on Goldie. Is his incomplete evidence deliberate, is he hiding something – or someone? The fact
that McQuinn is a policeman does not exclude him
from a fit of murderous rage.

Faro threw down his pen. Religious houses, he decided,
were naturally secretive places, a boon to prospective
murderers and the perfect settings for concealing evidence.
Secular staff were not permitted gentleman callers. Therefore all social activities of normal young unmarried women
who were not in holy orders had to be carried on *sub rosa*,
which made tracking down a murderer even more difficult.
Boarding schools were just a little behind convents in
natural reticence regarding their inmates.

Faro shuddered at the prospect of investigating a boys'
school. The headmaster, he expected, would be equally
uncooperative as the Reverend Mother – and for good
reason. His school might be tainted by association, however
obscure, with a murder. If one of his pupils had been in
contact with the murdered woman, then the headmaster
wouldn't wish to know officially, and would certainly resist,
with every means in his power, any attempt to make this
insalubrious association public knowledge.

Reading through the account again, Faro underlined the
Mad Baronet. He lived within easy access of the convent,
and Lily Goldie had been known to visit Solomon's Tower.
Unlikely as it seemed at first thought, this line of enquiry,
which had not been investigated, thanks to McQuinn's
apparent incompetence, might be pursued with profit.

He did not wait up for Vince that night. He did not
want to hear all he had missed, and a ravishing account of
Alison Aird as Lady Macbeth. He was relieved, too, when
Vince did not appear for breakfast, having left a note for
Mrs Brook that he had retired very late and wished to sleep
on undisturbed.

CHAPTER NINE

On arrival at the Central Office, Faro was handed the description he had been waiting for:

> Aged between eighteen and twenty-four. Five-foot-two in height. Curly red hair, several front teeth missing, body in poor condition, shows evidence of under-nourishment, in fourth month of pregnancy. No marks of violence. Death by drowning.

Obviously a suicide, unless she had been taken out in a boat and pushed into the river. Could this poor creature have been Clara Burnleigh, and had pregnancy been her reason for running away?

At the convent, the Reverend Mother received him with even less grace than the first time, if that were possible. Staring out of the window, drumming her fingers impatiently on the desk, she listened tight-lipped to his account of the visit to Fairmilehead.

'I have no other information than what I gave you, Inspector. I am not concealing evidence, if that is what you think, to protect the reputation of the convent, which, alas, thanks to police meddling, seems unlikely to survive these shattering blows.'

Cutting short his apologies, she demanded, 'And now, Inspector, what is it you wish me to do?'

Explaining that the body of a woman had been washed up

at Cramond, he asked, 'Could you identify Miss Burnleigh from this description?'

Reading quickly, she pushed it aside with distaste. 'Whoever this unfortunate creature is, she is certainly not Clara Burnleigh. There is not the slightest resemblance. Miss Burnleigh is very tall, with blonde straight hair, and she has excellent teeth.'

'You are quite sure?'

'Sure, Inspector? I am positive. My eyesight is excellent and Miss Burnleigh was a particular favourite of mine – and, I would add, a girl of the highest moral principles. I cannot imagine that she would have allowed herself to join the ranks of fallen women or to commit the sin of self-destruction.'

There remained the Mad Baronet, or, to give him his proper name, Sir Hedley Marsh. Faro realised that there was much to be gained from an apparently accidental meeting, an informal chat, rather than a rush to the door with all the appearance of officialdom. He decided to keep a close watch on Solomon's Tower and the behaviour of its owner, behaviour that belonged more to the early days of constables patrolling on duty, to 'watching and warding' rather than criminal investigation.

At the local dairy, on pretence of being a cat-lover, he was soon informed that the Mad Baronet received his delivery for his score of cats by six o'clock. Faro suspected that, in common with many old people, the Mad Baronet rose early, and he decided to be passing the gate, on a 'constitutional' himself, when the milk was taken indoors.

As he lingered, the pale morning mist enfolded and chilled him. It brought back memories of his early days on the Force. Suddenly he felt old – too old for the job. Recent illness had so weakened him that it seemed to have destroyed not only his appetite but also his self-confidence. Once upon a time, before Lizzie died, he had been hopeful, believed in the immortal soul of man, and his job of dealing with crimes and criminals had never destroyed his faith in human nature, for he had discovered that, in even the worst of them, the good seed, microscopic perhaps, still flourished and could be encouraged to grow.

When he had said this to Vince, the boy had laughed at him. 'Good heavens, Stepfather, surely those are not the requisites for a good detective. You would have made priest or minister with such feelings – quite Christ-like and forgiving. Well, I never.'

Faro had laughed. 'And you, dear lad, had you not chosen medicine, would have made an admirable detective.'

His thoughts were interrupted by the door of Solomon's Tower being thrown open as an avalanche of cats of all shapes, sizes, ages and conditions descended into the garden in the direction of the large milk churn at the gate. He was banking on the Mad Bart appearing himself. Having no servant was always something of a problem.

If there had been a maid, he thought, I could have enlisted Vince's help and, with an elaborate pretence of admiring her fine eyes, flattered her into giving information. Even a fine sturdy coachman might have been wheedled by flattery – such splendid horses. But a baronet, mad or sane, who is also a hermit – there's a plaguey difficult situation.

He did not have long to wait. The last of the cats were followed by a shambling figure, immensely tall and, despite hooded white hair and beard, Faro got an impression that he was strong still and powerfully built. It was, in fact, thanks to a piece of haddock retrieved from last night's supper that Faro had succeeded in gaining the attention of a handsome ginger tom, who leaped through the railings and bolted down the juicy morsel, giving polite thanks by an immediate caressing of Faro's ankles.

'A fine fellow you have here.'

The hooded figure scowled and pretended not to hear. 'Come in at once, Boxer. At once, sir.'

'Boxer, is that your name?' said Faro, addressing the cat.
'You're a fine chap. And so friendly— '

'Immediately, I said!' was the shout from inside the gate,
and Boxer departed somewhat reluctantly.

'I say – sir . . .' shouted Faro, looking through the
railings.

'What is it?'

'I don't suppose you'd have a kitten you could spare –
to sell, I mean, to a good home?'

The Mad Bart scowled and cast an eye over his brood.
'Depends.'

'My housekeeper is a great cat-lover, and we're smitten
with a plague of mice – these new houses, you know.'

'Mice, is it? There hasn't been a mouse inside these walls
for more years than I can remember.'

As he considered Faro in the manner of one about to
sell a favourite daughter, the latter said hastily, 'I would
willingly pay you. I'm sorry if I've offended you by my
question but we are at our wits' end, and as I often see your
cats in the garden when I'm out walking, I thought . . .'

'I don't need payment,' said the old man huffily. 'Wouldn't
consider it. Have plenty of kits to spare, never miss the odd
one.' He paused again and stared hard at Faro in the manner
of one about to make a momentous decision. 'Er, perhaps
you'd care to step inside and look at 'em. Have some in the
kitchen ready to leave their mother.'

This was better luck than Faro had hoped for as, leading
the way, the old man apologised for the untidiness, which
was not immediately evident. Apart from the offensive
odour of cat *en masse*, the house was surprisingly clean
and tidy for an old man living on his own and lacking
servants.

'Can I offer you some refreshment? A dram, perhaps?
No?'

Faro watched the old man pour out whisky from a
decanter. Lighting his pipe was a lengthy operation, so it

was some time before the conversation resumed.

'Only use a couple of rooms these days, one for the cats, one for myself.' Down the long stone corridor lay the kitchen, which smelt rather worse than the rest of the house, and Faro was careful not to breathe too deeply. However, the kittens were exceedingly pretty.

'I don't know how to decide which one,' said Faro in all honesty. 'Perhaps my housekeeper would be better able— '

'Women are no judges of a good mouser. Here, take this one. Comes of a good mouser strain. Take my word for it, you'll have no more trouble.' As Faro put his hand in his pocket, the old man added sternly, 'As a gift – I insist. I want no money. Can't keep 'em all. Have to be cruel to be kind sometimes,' he added. 'Drown a whole litter occasionally. Better that way than putting 'em out to run wild. Place would be overrun . . .'

Faro could see no valid reason for refusing the offer, and hoped he had not let himself in for Mrs Brook's displeasure, seeing the mouse plague had been a pure piece of invention and he had not the least idea whether the housekeeper was a cat-lover or not. He was considering by what means he could extend the interview when the Mad Bart suddenly said, 'I know you. You're that detective chap. You live across in the new houses.'

'That is correct,' said Faro weakly. 'How did you know?'

'Girl who came to visit my cats, from the convent, told me who you were.'

'Girl?'

'You know, one who was murdered – second one. Teacher. Heard about it. Grocer lad told me. Most unfortunate.'

'So you knew her?'

The Mad Bart looked vague. 'No more than I know you, sir. As I said, saw my cats. Took a notion to buying one. Mice in her room, too. Scared of 'em. Pleasant girl, kind

94

too. Was suffering from one of my attacks of the ague at the time. Told me the nuns made a good concoction of herbs. Brought some. Papist muck, of course, but did the trick. Never saw her again.' His accompanying sigh, a shake of the great shaggy head, more than any words gave a glimpse of the loneliness of his life. 'No. Never saw her again,' he repeated sadly. 'Rotten business. Glad they got the fellow. Deserved to swing for it. *Crime passionnel*, was it?'

'I don't think so,' said Faro vaguely, anxious not to divert the stream of confidence.

'Oh, thought he had led her on, let her down. Damn fool. Had I been younger, I'd have married her myself.'

Suddenly feeling that he was getting valuable information at last, Faro's senses were on the alert. Had the cats been Lily Goldie's excuse for an introduction to the Mad Bart? Had she perhaps had an eye on marrying this mad old man? The idea wasn't as impossible as it first seemed. It was happening every day, girls who married men old enough to be their grandfathers, for the money and, more often, for the title.

'This chap – wasn't the one she hoped to marry then?'

'Not as far as we know. That didn't come out in the evidence, anyway,' said Faro cautiously.

'I naturally presumed . . .'

'Presumed?'

'From what she said, that there was someone . . .'

Faro felt a surge of excitement. So there was a man in existence who had offered Lily Goldie marriage.

'Didn't you tell anyone about this?'

'Why should I? Wasn't any of my business. After all, they got her murderer, didn't they?' He looked at Faro for a moment before continuing. 'Can tell you who it was she hoped to marry, though. If you're interested. That young chap who fell under a train. Turned out that her expectations came to nothing, fellow was penniless, bit of a waster. Sent him packing. Quite right, seeing he had been leading her on. Not the done thing for a gentleman, is it now?'

Faro looked bleak. It had cost this particular young gentleman his life. 'So you didn't consider the police should be told.'

'If anyone had come and asked me, I should have told them. For what it was worth.'

Leaving the kitchen with the kitten miaowing plaintively in its cardboard box, Faro silently cursed McQuinn as the Mad Bart said, 'My felicitations to your young constable. Enjoys a chat over my garden wall when he's on duty. Gather he was brought up by nuns, or some such background. Don't hold that against him even if he is a papist. He's a shrewd young fellow. He'll go far, mark my words. Can all rest easy in our beds, knowing we have such chaps in the police.'

As they shook hands at the door, Faro went away feeling sourly that wherever he went these days McQuinn seemed to have been there first, covering his inefficiency by ingratiating himself with everyone, from nuns to mad baronets. And managing very conveniently to be first on the scene at Cramond Island when the drowned girl was washed ashore.

Faro hoped his feelings were natural ones for having been thwarted by the case of Lily Goldie and not allowed to complete his own thorough investigations. He didn't like McQuinn but he didn't want to fall into a trap he knew of from experience of older detectives, eager to blame young constables for their own failures and mistakes. He also felt a question had been posed to which he must, by tact or guile, find the answer: what did Danny McQuinn know of Lily Goldie's personal life that had failed to find its way into his reports?

'So much for our private investigations,' he told Vince over supper that evening, a delighted Mrs Brook having taken the pretty ginger kitten into custody.

Vince looked thoughtful. 'Are you sure that's all the Mad Bart said?'

Faro was hurt. He prided himself on his remarkable memory and the ability to make verbatim reports of conversations where necessary. 'I am sure. Obviously the old gentleman was correct in assuming that Ferris had told Lily he was well off – until he was disinherited, or whatever, after failing his exams.'

Vince sighed. 'On the other hand, she might have been telling our Mad Bart that to keep him at a distance. There's no fool like an old fool in love.' His mocking glance in his stepfather's direction made Faro wince. He refused, however, to fall for that particular piece of bait, and Vince continued, 'Surely if there had been a man involved who loved her honourably and wanted to marry her he would have appeared at Hymes's trial?'

'Only if he was innocent of her murder.'

'You mean, you think that he's the man we're looking for? A Mr X about whom we know nothing but who, for reasons we will never know, might have murdered Lily Goldie? Well, who is he, and, more important, where is he? Tantalising, isn't it?'

'Something to hide doesn't make him guilty of murder. Perhaps his crime was being a philanderer, a bit of a bounder who gained Lily Goldie's favours under false pretences, like Ferris. Or our Mr X might have been married already, in which case he would consider it prudent not to draw undue attention to himself and his extra-marital activities. Or, if he wasn't married, he and Lily could have quarrelled violently. She could have been blackmailing him – anything – there could be some very good reasons why he might not have wanted to appear at a murder trial.'

From his own vast experience of crimes and criminal trials, Faro was fully aware that anyone who so appears, however innocent, is immediately besmirched in the public eye. Respectable Edinburgh society would go far to avoid 'that man who appeared at the notorious murder trial'. Faro also knew that such a notoriety was one that most men would go far to assiduously avoid, even to concealing vital evidence.

'You know, I still incline to our Mad Bart,' said Vince, 'as the most hopeful suspect. Tell me about his hands.'

'His hands?'

'Yes. Did you notice anything about them?'

'Only that they were crippled with rheumatism.'

'That's it,' said Vince triumphantly. 'I thought they would be, because what little I've seen of him walking, his feet are also affected.'

'Small wonder, living in that wretchedly damp tower.'

'Did he have difficulty using his hands?'

'As a matter of fact, yes. Pouring out a dram, lighting his pipe, took him a long time. Obviously, the pressure needed for strangulation would be beyond him.'

'There you are. That's it,' repeated Vince. 'Don't you see, Stepfather? You're missing the whole point. What did I tell you right at the beginning?'

'That Lily was pushed off the Crags . . .'

'And the scarf tied about her neck afterwards, to make it look the same as the Hymes murder.' Seeing Faro's doubtful expression, he sighed. 'Well, if it wasn't the Mad Bart with his rheumaticky hands, who are we left with?'

Faro rubbed his chin thoughtfully. 'Hands incapable of strangling could also apply to a woman.'

'A woman?'

'Yes. I'm giving serious consideration to the missing and mysterious Miss Clara Burnleigh.'

'Are you now? Well, it's a deuced interesting theory.'

'It poses only one question. Why?'

'Jealousy is the most obvious reason. But we can't know for sure until we track her down. And that I'm quite determined on.'

'Dead or alive?'

'Hopefully alive. Because at least we know that Miss Burnleigh isn't the poor unfortunate lying in the mortuary, and the chances are that she is very much alive and not too far away.'

Next morning, when Faro went to the Central Office, Constable McQuinn was waiting to give him a message.

'The drowned girl, sir. Her parents came and identified her late last night. Here are the papers.' The statement said little, but McQuinn was eager to fill in the details. 'Terrible state the mother was in – usual thing. Father showed the girl the door when he knew she was pregnant. Advocate, pillar of the Church, very respectable and all that sort of thing. Suicide it was, just as I thought when I first saw the corpse. Poor girl, with no one to turn to, threw herself in the river.'

A waste of a life, thought Faro. It was the story of so many young girls. But what was left to them? A back-street abortion and a painful death in all probability. Or, if they and the child survived as outcasts from society, the woman bringing up her child alone, with not the least hope that any respectable man would wish to marry her, often resorted to prostitution as the only means of earning a living where her past would not be held against her.

'There is another letter for you, sir. Came by last night's post.'

Faro tore open the envelope. In black capital letters the message read, 'Clara B. is a lying whore. So was her mother. Try asking for them beyond the crossroads at Mrs Wishart's.' It was signed, 'One Who Seeks Justice'.

As he hailed a cab from the stance at Parliament House, where several vehicles were reserved for police use, Faro felt triumphant. His visit to Fairmilehead had seriously upset some person or persons who bore Clara Burnleigh and her mother a grudge. From such disagreeable sources, information was readily forthcoming and eagerly given.

This was the break that all detectives longed for and seldom received. He felt the sure tingle of excitement that within hours the mystery of the missing Clara Burnleigh would be resolved.

He would be one step nearer to discovering the identity of Lily Goldie's slayer, and apprehending the second murderer.

CHAPTER TEN

As the hired gig drove at a smart pace through villages and fields and smoky hamlets towards Fairmilehead, Faro found his thoughts returning to Alison Aird. He wished he had not decided to make this second visit alone. The day was identical in weather to that first excursion with her and it intensified his longing to see her again.

At every stage of the journey, Faro was haunted by Alison's presence: here we laughed at the children playing with a kitten; here she quoted *Hamlet*; here we admired an old water-mill.

The sun disappeared, a chill wind came leaping out of the Pentlands and cut across his shoulders like a cold knife. The walk was sad, as if she was dead and had left him for ever. He could hardly believe that at this moment she was probably sitting happily in her lodgings, sipping tea and going over her script for the next play in the repertoire. He had to steel himself and remember that he had not lost her, that the battle had not yet begun: a battle still to fight is also a battle still to win.

As he opened the gate of Mrs Wishart's residence, which to his relief he found without difficulty, Alison's smiling ghost retreated as the detective swept aside the sentimental would-be lover.

What if there was no one at home and his journey fruitless? The old house stood aloof and shrouded by trees, a short distance from the village. Its windows and front door, its neat garden, spoke of shabby gentility. His second summons brought forth a response and the door was opened by a maid, whose appearance was in keeping with the house. She looked as if she had been serving in the establishment for some considerable time.

'Mrs Wishart?'

'Who wants her?'

'Who is it, what do you want?' An old lady peered over the maid's shoulder. 'We are not at home today.'

'Mrs Wishart?'

'That is my name.' She regarded him, frowning, and he half expected the same reluctance as he had received, a stranger, at the Mad Bart's door. He was soon to discover that her manner was due to deafness rather than hostility.

'I wonder, madam, if you can help me. I'm looking for a young lady. She, er, calls herself Clara Burnleigh.'

'I will deal with this. Go you back to your work.' And dismissing the maid, Mrs Wishart asked him to repeat the question. At the name, she gave a rather violent start.

'I thought that was what you said.' A faint shadow disturbed the serene face, a slight hesitation. 'I know no one of that name.'

'That is a pity. I was advised to make my enquiry to you.'

'Indeed. And who wishes to know?'

Faro decided in his turn to be deaf, and said, 'Burnleigh may not be her real name, but I have good reason to believe she comes from this area. A tall pretty girl with fair straight hair,' he added, remembering the Reverend Mother's description.

The old lady nodded vigorously, as if the description tallied. Then, examining Faro through her lorgnette, she demanded, 'And who might you be?'

'Before I tell you my name, let me say that I only wish to talk to the young lady about one of her friends. An unfortunate colleague who was murdered— '

'Murdered – but how horrible. Horrible.'

'A Miss Lily Goldie. Perhaps you knew of her?'

'No. No. As for Clara, I'm not aware . . .' The old woman stopped, confused, her lips suddenly tight closed.

'Aware?' Faro asked.

'What Clara can do to help you with your enquiries. Justice has been done. I read in the newspapers that the murderer was hanged – weeks ago.'

'That is so. But I am here to conduct a private investigation at the behest of a relative,' Faro lied cheerfully. 'This is an absolutely confidential matter and nothing you care to tell me need go any further.'

Mrs Wishart accepted the implication that the relative was one of Lily Goldie's. 'In that case, of course, of course, I will do what I can to help you. Come inside.'

As had been suggested by the exterior, the interior was spick and span and comfortably if plainly furnished.

'Do sit down, Mr . . .?'

'Faro.'

'You will take some tea?' After ringing the bell for the maid, she said, 'What I am about to tell you is in the very strictest confidence, and I rely on your discretion as a gentleman— '

'Before you do so, I ought to tell you that I am a detective inspector – in this case acting in a private capacity.'

'I see no reason why there should not be gentlemen among policemen.' She gave him a shrewd glance. 'I have lived a long time, Inspector Faro, and whatever your profession you have the look of a man I would trust.'

The maid brought in tea, and when it was served Mrs Wishart continued, 'Burnleigh is not Clara's real name. That is her mother's name and was mine before I married. Clara is my grand-niece. Her real name is Clerkwell.' She paused. 'There was a great scandal attached to that name about fifteen years ago. Perhaps you remember it?'

'Of course. A case of embezzlement and— '

'And Clara's mother was deeply involved with the partner in the firm. You know the rest.'

It had been before his time, but was a *cause célèbre* in the records of the Edinburgh City Police. Clerkwell had been cheated by his stepbrother and had committed suicide – a suicide in such suspicious circumstances that it was very probably murder dressed up to look as if Clerkwell had taken his own life. Ethel Clerkwell was tried and acquitted with the verdict: Not Proven.

'The poor child, my grand-niece, lived under the stigma of all that implied in Edinburgh society.'

Faro smiled grimly. Not Proven was a byword with the magistrates. We know you did it, but we can't prove it. Go away and don't do it again.

'Her mother's life was shattered by the scandal. Her health never recovered and Clara had nursed her devotedly. Imagine a child of ten, hardly understanding anything but the terrible cloud that hovered over her mother's reason. By the time the child was eighteen, it looked as if poor Ethel would have to be committed to an insane asylum. But Clara stayed with her until, mercifully, two years ago she died. Clara was heartbroken but free. They had long since reverted to the name of Burnleigh, and it was under that name she sought a situation as a teacher in an Edinburgh convent – I cannot remember the name.'

Faro told her, and asked, 'Did the sisters know her story?'

Mrs Wishart shook her head. 'No. As I told you, she wished to begin a completely new life. She told no one. A year ago, she met a young man of property, well connected in Edinburgh society. They fell in love and he asked her to marry him. She was in something of a dilemma, poor child, for she was afraid that by telling him the truth she would lose him. While she was summoning up her courage, one of the maids was murdered. The police came to investigate and my poor Clara was horrified, guiltily aware that they might well discover the truth about her on the eve of her marriage, which she had kept secret even from the sisters. And so she fled.'

Mrs Wishart paused to refill Faro's teacup. 'I have to tell you that Clara's story has a happy ending. The young man's regard for her was in no way diminished by her revelations. Her story merely strengthened the depth of his love and determination to cherish her as his wife. If you wish, I can ask her if she would be willing to speak to you, privately, of course.'

'If you would be so good. I will give you my address.'

'That will not be necessary, Inspector. She lives not far away – in the next village. Her husband is not at home, alas, a family bereavement has him in Stirling this week. Clara was unable to accompany him for reasons of health.'

'She is ailing?'

Mrs Wishart smiled fondly. 'Shall we say, they have expectations of a happy event and the early stages are somewhat trying?'

'Perhaps I should not intrude upon her at this time?'

'By this hour of the day, the worst will be over. It is only in the mornings when she feels considerably unwell and would be unlikely to feel strong enough to receive a visitor.'

As he pocketed Clara's card and prepared to take his leave, Faro said, 'You have been very helpful, Mrs Wishart. I trust that your grand-niece will receive me as graciously.'

'I think you have my word for that. My poor Clara, having suffered so greatly herself, has learned the lesson early in life, that we should be willing to help others in distress. And this unhappy relative of poor Miss Goldie?' she enquired, inviting further explanation. When this was not forthcoming, she went on, 'My grand-niece has a kind heart. I am sure she will receive you.'

On the doorstep, Faro turned and thanked her once again.

'One moment, Inspector. There is one question you might be good enough to answer – to satisfy my curiosity.'

'And that is?'

'Who gave you my name? I ask because it appears that our secret is not as well hidden as we imagined.'

Faro considered and decided against revealing the scurrilous letter. 'It came without any signature. Do you have an enemy, Mrs Wishart?' he added gently.

The old lady was unperturbed. 'Perhaps everyone has, Inspector. Resentments, old slights, fester through the years in small villages. There were those who were jealous of Clara's good marriage.'

Faro worked on the well-worn principle that there is much to be gained from the element of surprise, namely, the unexpected visit. He knew from long experience that those first minutes are crucial, for it is then more than at any other time that, to the detective's shrewd and observant eye, guilt is revealed or innocence proclaimed without a word being exchanged.

Clara Denbridge, née Burnleigh, lived but two miles away from her great-aunt, and Faro once again left the cab in a convenient lane at a discreet distance from the house. It was a pleasant sunny day and he enjoyed the walk with its prospect of Edinburgh Castle like a great grey ship sailing on the far horizon. Mellowed by distance, it became the castle from a fairy tale. Hard to believe that beyond those great trees and hidden villages lay a thriving bustling city of commerce, a city where every stone was steeped in a bloody history of battles and violence.

Faro sighed. And it seemed to get worse rather than better as the centuries progressed. If there was a lesson to be taken from history, it was that men lived but never learned from the mistakes of the past.

The Denbridge residence was in the modern baronial style, bristling with pepperpot turrets, in blatant imitation of the ruined old castle which frowned down upon it from the hillside. Set in an attractive garden, along an impressive drive with a coach-house, its air of opulence was completed by the trimly uniformed maid who opened the door.

From her slightly flustered, anxious appearance, Faro deduced even before she opened her mouth that she was a local lass, bursting with pride at having a smart new uniform as she twitched at cap and pinafore. Her eagerness to be helpful suggested that she had not been long in her present employment, or, judging by her extreme youth, in any employment at all. It also suggested that the Denbridges had not been long established and had few visitors.

To his question she said, 'The mistress. Oh yes, she's at home – I mean, I'll see, if you'll just wait a wee minute.' Then, turning in her tracks, she remembered the essential, 'Who shall I say is calling?'

Faro took a chance. 'A friend of her great-aunt, Mrs Wishart from Fairmilehead.'

Clara Denbridge appeared with the alacrity of one who had been lurking in the hall. She almost thrust the maid aside in her eagerness to confront Faro.

'Mrs Wishart? Is there something wrong – is she ill?'

Her anxiety indicated the devotion that existed between them, and hastily he put her mind at rest.

'No, Mrs Denbridge. She was in excellent health and spirits when I left her a little while ago.'

Clara sighed. 'Oh, that is good. I was afraid . . .' Calm again, she waited, smiling politely.

'Detective Inspector Faro.'

At the name, her hand flew to her lips. Dread filled her eyes as she whispered, 'The Inspector who came to the convent. What – what is your business with me?'

Indicating the servant, Faro said, 'Your maid holds the letter from Mrs Wishart which explains the reason for my visit.'

107

Hastily tearing open the envelope, Clara read the brief message. 'You had better come in. Annie,' she called in the direction of the kitchen. 'Tea, if you please.'

The parlour into which he was ushered continued the opulence suggested by the exterior. There seemed to be not one possession in that room which was any older than the young bride herself. Everything spoke of proud new ownership. Paintings, ornaments, silver, a rich but not necessarily matching assortment and some half-unwrapped parcels suggested recently acquired wedding presents. From the room itself came the lingering smells of paint, and the upholstery, cushions, sofas and carpets added that indefinable but not unpleasant odour of new wool. Anti-macassars and curtains were of fine linen and even the furniture smelt as if the wood from which it was constructed was within living memory of a pine forest.

'Do please sit down, Inspector Faro.'

As he did so, Clara swept aside two of the parcels and apologised for the untidiness. 'We have only been installed in the house since we returned from honeymoon a month ago and, alas, the promised bookcases have failed to put in an appearance. My – my husband,' she continued, a pretty blush declaring that the title was not yet well used by her, 'my husband and I are both great readers.'

Faro smiled. 'Please don't apologise. I have just moved into my new home six months ago, and as both my step-son and I acquire a considerable number of books – he is a newly graduated doctor – we have similar problems. It is good of you to receive me, madam, at such a time, with such short notice.'

'I presume your business is urgent, or else my great-aunt would not have sent you. She is most reliable in such matters. Is there something I can do for you? Is it about poor Lily Goldie?'

Faro explained that this was a routine visit on behalf of a

relative of Lily Goldie. 'After my first visit to Fairmilehead, I feared that there might have been some less agreeable reason for your disappearance.'

'I behaved foolishly,' interrupted Mrs Denbridge, 'and I apologise for putting you to so much trouble and speculation, Inspector. It did not occur to me that I would be inconveniencing anyone by my story. As my great-aunt will have told you, I felt it necessary at the time. Thankfully, that is no longer the case.'

'I can only say that I am delighted for you.'

Clara smiled. 'I fear I can say little that will help you, which is a great shame, you having come all this way. Lily and I had the merest acquaintance. She was a naturally secretive person and I'm afraid she had to do a great deal more listening to my troubles at the time – I was too pre-occupied with my imminent marriage to pay a great deal of attention to her activities.'

'Our enquiries revealed that she had a sweetheart, a possible suitor,' said Faro boldly, taking a chance. 'Is that correct?'

'Why, yes. Such a tragedy. Did you not know?' she added in a hushed voice. 'The poor unfortunate gentleman fell' (the word was heavily emphasised) 'under a train.'

Faro made sympathetic noises and handed her the photograph. 'Do you recognise him?'

'Of course. That is a very good likeness of Mr Ferris.'

'You met him then?'

'A fleeting acquaintance. Hardly that, even, for Lily seemed very anxious to avoid a formal introduction,' she added, with a touch of pique.

'For what reason, Mrs Denbridge?'

Clara shrugged delicately. 'Many young women do not care to introduce their suitors. It is a disagreeable and very impolite trait and it implies that they are afraid of competition. I mean— '

'I see exactly what you mean.'

'Let us be frank, Inspector. For all her bragging of her conquests, Lily was not at all certain of Mr Ferris's intentions. I knew she wished to be married but I gathered there was some impediment to this marriage. I remember her saying that she would have to work on him. "I shall have to use all my woman's wiles if I am to get him to the altar, Clara." I remember, those were her very words. However, one cannot repeat confidences of this nature.' She put her hands together primly. 'I do not in the least wish to talk ill of the dead, of Lily or poor Mr Ferris, but I felt that, er, they had misbehaved.'

'Misbehaved?'

'Yes, Inspector.' Clara blushed. 'As a married woman, I can only suggest that they had been on – er, terms of intimacy.'

'For what reason?' Faro demanded sharply.

Clara shook her head. 'I cannot say more, except that females sharing rooms know certain things about each other rather by instinct than any conversation, which, of course, would be highly improper.'

'I do wish you had told me about this at the time.'

'I was unmarried myself, and somewhat embarrassed. Besides,' she added righteously, 'ladies do not readily cast aspersions upon a colleague's character, especially when she has been murdered, Inspector. And as it seemed that her murderer – the wicked man Hymes – had been apprehended, I guessed that he had been responsible and that was the reason why he had murdered her.'

'Responsible?'

'Yes, indeed, Inspector. You see . . .' She took a deep breath and continued. 'I knew – by certain things – female things, after he died – that she suspected she was – er – in trouble.'

'Do I take your meaning that Miss Goldie had reason to believe she was carrying a child?' said Faro bluntly.

'Yes,' whispered Clara. '"His parents – someone – will have to pay for this little indiscretion." Those were her very words, Inspector. You can imagine how difficult it was for me. Had I announced my suspicions, it would have been a blow to the convent's reputation and I would have been merely blackening her character even further, if my suspicions were not correct. Having suffered deeply from the scurrilous slanders of heartless people – I saw my own mother destroyed by such slanders, remember that, Inspector – I could never have forgiven myself. And it appears I would have been wrong, for there was no mention of what I suspected at the trial. Perhaps you can tell me, Inspector, was I correct?'

'The post-mortem on Lily Goldie revealed no such evidence that could besmirch her character.'

'Then I am greatly relieved.'

'You believe, then, that Hymes was responsible for her murder?'

'I see no reason to doubt it. Perhaps she was desperate.'

'Desperate?'

'Yes. She believed she had to find a father for the child. Anyone who would give it a name and save her reputation.'

'But Hymes was married already.'

'I don't suppose Lily knew that.'

'I'm sorry, Mrs Denbridge, but what you are suggesting simply does not make sense.'

'It makes good sense to me, or to any woman who finds herself in such a situation. You have my assurances on that, Inspector,' she added sharply.

'Surely you would think it strange that such a – lady – as Miss Goldie appeared to be, should have formed an attachment with Hymes in the first place?'

'Not if she was desperate to find a husband in her unhappy circumstances. Besides, perhaps he had some fearful fascination for her, even mesmeric,' she added,

111

eyes gleaming. 'This, I understand, can happen all too often when young ladies emerge from sheltered lives and allow themselves to be preyed upon by creatures from the lower classes.'

Clara's conclusions certainly threw some unusual light on Lily Goldie's activities, and on the ways of womankind in general, thought Faro cynically. As a detective used to dealing in facts, he found it almost impossible to give credence to such an imaginative explanation.

As he was leaving, Faro glanced over the notes he had written. 'When Miss Goldie expressed her fears of being pregnant, did I understand that she said to you: "His parents – or someone – will have to pay dearly for this little indiscretion"?'

'Yes, indeed. Those were her words. I am positive.'

'I merely put it to you that you might have been mistaken, because Ferris was an orphan.'

Clara laughed. 'Now, Inspector, it is you who are mistaken. Tim had a young brother at St Leonard's.'

'You are sure of that?'

'Of course I am. I met him with Lily on two occasions. He's about fourteen or fifteen. Rather slightly built, but a handsome boy, with fine features, from what I could see, as he did not have the courtesy to raise his cap to me. Of course, I understood, it's an awkward age and he was obviously very shy and ill-at-ease.'

'What was his name?'

Clara spread her hands wide. 'Inspector, I have the most appalling memory for names – I even forget those of people to whom I'm introduced, which can be most embarrassing. And in this case, I doubt whether I would have considered Tim's young brother important enough to have it stick in my mind.'

'One more question, Mrs Denbridge, if you will oblige. Did these meetings take place before or after Mr Ferris died?'

112

Clara bit her lip. 'About the same time. Yes, I remember thinking it very appropriate, and hoping that Lily was a comfort to Tim's brother in his sad loss.'

As he said his farewells, Faro added, 'If the boy's name should come to mind – or any other detail, however trivial it seems to you, I would be most obliged if you would drop me a note. Here is my private address.'

He rejoined the cab, whose driver was enjoying a quiet snooze in the sunshine. On the way back to Edinburgh, Faro decided that the meeting with Clara Burnleigh now presented him with what he most dreaded: a visit to St Leonard's. First of all, he must explain his reasons to the Headmaster, who might not be kindly disposed towards having a detective inspector interview Ferris Minor.

Faro sighed. For a dead man, Timothy Ferris was turning out to be persistently enigmatic. The only remaining hope was that his young brother would shed some light on a particularly baffling case. And one which he now regretted having reopened.

If only he could believe in Clara Burnleigh's reasoning, absurd as it was, and accept that Lily Goldie had given Hymes good reason for murdering her.

If only, to quote Superintendent Mackintosh, he had 'let hanged murderers lie'.

CHAPTER ELEVEN

At the Central Office, there were no new cases for him, merely a routine check on Wormwoodhall to establish the whereabouts of the notorious Black Tam, whose re-entry into society had produced a spate of robberies with violence.

As St Leonard's School lay on the respectable area bordering Causewayside, he might be able to catch Black Tam and interview Ferris Minor in one visit. It was an appealing thought and, closing his door, Faro put up his feet on his desk, sent out for a pint of porter and, for the first time in months, a mutton pie. Then he sat down and, sharpening a pen, drew up a sheet of paper and compiled a complete report from his sketchy notes of his meeting with Clara Burnleigh.

He wondered what Vince would make of his findings as he set off for St Leonard's, a modern building despite its aggressively medieval castellations. The long drive, not yet decently shaded by trees, seemed oddly naked, the house deserted.

'There's no one here,' said a gardener. 'The whole school is away on a founder's day picnic to Peebles.'

Faro thanked him for the information and left. Heading for Causewayside led him past the street where Alison Aird lodged with the other female members of Trelawney's Thespians.

Why not call upon her? His excuse was feeble but

irresistible, an apology for having missed her performance in *Macbeth*.

Mrs Penny, the landlady, eyed him sourly. 'Mrs Aird is not at home.' And without any further question, she added, 'I do not know where she has gone, and I do not know when she will return. And I am unable to take messages of any kind for my boarders. That is my rule. You may leave a note on the hall table, if you so desire.'

Faro regarded the formidable lady with awe. Large, florid, her face painted, and doubtless wearing a discarded theatrical wig of a suspiciously youthful gold. As she spoke, Mrs Penny's appearance suggested the figurehead of a ship come to grotesque life.

And one well able to repel boarders, thought Faro, making his apologies and his way to the gate, under her keen eye. A lady who would take no nonsense from anyone.

He continued on his way into the warrens of Causewayside, with a certain caution and reluctance. He was already known to many of the inhabitants, for he had regularly appeared to run famous criminals to earth in this notorious area.

The cobbled street was quite crowded, but as he walked down, trying to maintain an air of jaunty indifference, most of the inhabitants melted into the shadows of the grimy tenements and dingy hovels. By the time the Quaker Mission came into view, the street was almost deserted and he guessed that word of his coming had already spread like wildfire among the thieves and vagabonds whose presence had sorely tried him in the past.

The mission was situated in a secluded court with a tiny garden. He had never set foot in it before, but Alison Aird's association with the Quakers made him curious, and as he looked inside he thought he saw her sitting under a tree, and reading from a book to an audience of small children.

Could it be? She was against the sun, but yes, it was indeed Alison Aird. He stood in the shadows, for a moment

115

enjoying the contrast between her gentle beauty, her muslin frock and neat hair, and the grimy poverty of the ragged urchins, bare-limbed, filthy, verminous. The sight struck his heart with new tenderness and an overwhelming desire to protect her.

She was unaware of his presence until his shadow came between her and the sun. The children's reaction was immediate – 'Scarper. Peelers.' – and they melted into the distance before she had finished reading the sentence.

'Children? Come back here – what on earth . . .?'

Turning, she saw his tall figure approaching across the grass. She stood up and held out her hand with a welcoming smile – but no more.

'Good day, Inspector.' She frowned. 'This is very unexpected.'

'Not at all, Mrs Aird. This is a neighbourhood which I unfortunately know very well indeed.'

'What brings you here? You have not come to arrest me, I hope?'

Faro laughed at her bewilderment. 'I have come in search of a gentleman known as Black Tam. But I suspect that news of my approach has already reached him.'

'Is he a dangerous character?'

'Very.'

'Then are you wise to come alone?'

Her anxious tone suggested concern. Did she really care? he thought. 'What of yourself, Mrs Aird? I see you have not heeded my advice.'

'Will you be reassured if I tell you that I come armed?'

'Armed?'

'Yes, Inspector, armed.' Despite her solemn tones, he had an uneasy suspicion that she was laughing at him. From her reticule she withdrew a tiny dagger from a jewelled sheath. 'I go nowhere without it.' Handing it to Faro, she continued, 'It was a present from an Indian holy man long ago who said that one day it would protect me from a terrible death.'

Returning it, Faro did not add that it would be useless against a strong assailant. 'A pretty toy, Mrs Aird, but you would be better not to tempt fate and stay away from this area. As I have told you, it is no place for a gentlewoman.'

Mrs Aird laughed. 'As I told *you* before, I am no gentlewoman, merely an actress.' She held up the book of *Tales from Shakespeare*. 'I was asked by the Quakers if I would read to the poor children, in the hope that it might provide the right inspiration for them to make a better life for themselves.'

Faro refrained from commenting that it would take a great deal more than that to wean them away from the sordid existence that was bred in them, from first cry to dying breath.

'You look doubtful, Inspector. There is no danger here. The poor are not all wicked. Sometimes all they have to give is their friendship.'

He made a grimace. 'Not to policemen. And I would advise you, beware the face of innocence. It is most often a mask, and you have chosen to work in the midst of a strong criminal element.'

With a sigh, she closed her book, gathered up her bonnet and basket. 'Since you have scared away my little friends, I might as well return to my lodging. Would you care to accompany me? Mrs Penny will give us tea – her scones are delicious. Where has everyone disappeared to?' she whispered as they walked down the almost deserted street. 'I have never seen the place so empty. What on earth did you do to them, Inspector?'

'Nothing, I assure you. But they know my reputation. I rarely come to Wormwoodhall and leave again empty-handed.'

'Empty-handed? How so?'

117

'Yes. I usually take some member of their fraternity away with the cuffs about his wrists.'

'Good gracious, Inspector. You alarm me. You seemed such a friendly man, calm, full of compassion. I could not imagine you putting the fear of death into anyone. And now I am seeing you in a very different role. I feel quite cheated,' she added, with a mocking smile.

'We all have our obverse side, Mrs Aird.' And he thought of the grieving woman in grey he had first seen in Greyfriars Kirkyard and of his instant infatuation. While he wondered how he might with tact raise the subject of that first meeting, his senses were strangely aroused by her forearms under the parasol she carried. So soft and gently freckled, defenceless and utterly lovely, he longed to seize her in his arms.

Would her reaction be outrage, at being kissed in the public street, he thought, following her along the path to her lodgings where a transformed Mrs Penny greeted their arrival together.

Alison Aird was clearly a favourite and when she went upstairs to her bedroom to attend to her toilette, Mrs Penny, with the undisguised delight of a match-maker, now fawned upon the Inspector.

Full of eye-fluttering apologies for her harshness in sending him away, she whispered, 'So many admirers, and I have my instructions, directly from Mrs Aird: not to admit anyone. Those are her very words. In all the time she has been under my roof, she has never once brought a gentleman back to partake of my tea and scones until this moment.' She gave him an admiring glance. 'But the moment I saw you, I should have realised that you were different. That you were someone special. I do most abjectly apologise for my behaviour towards you, sir, and trust that it will be overlooked.'

Faro, feeling exceedingly flattered, readily agreed, where-upon Mrs Penny was at great pains to inform him that Mrs Aird was A Gem.

'She is the perfect boarder, sir, there are none to match her for gentleness and consideration. It will be a devastation, sir, to me personally, a devastation to lose her.'

'Who are you about to lose, Mrs Penny?' asked Mrs Aird, who had entered the room soft-footed having changed her sturdy outdoor shoes for slippers.

'Well, yourself, Mrs Aird. I was just remarking to the Inspector that I have prayed you would meet some nice gentleman who would persuade you to leave all those actors, and that uncertain life you have on the stage.'

Her bold look in Faro's direction was unmistakable, but Mrs Aird did not blush or look embarrassed, she merely shrugged and said, 'I fear not, Mrs Penny. I have no great wish to marry again and I have passed the age where I am likely to appeal to some eligible man who will sweep me off my feet and wish to have me as his life partner.'

This revelation did not please Faro. It merely emphasised what he already suspected – that his regard for Mrs Aird was by no means mutual. She obviously did not consider him an attractive proposition and had never thought of him in the role of prospective husband.

When they were alone with the tea and scones before them, Mrs Aird said, 'Did you return to Fairmilehead to find the missing lady?'

'I did. The reason for her apparent deception had an innocent explanation.'

'Did I not tell you so? Was I not right?' asked Mrs Aird triumphantly.

'In part, yes.' And Faro was suddenly aware that a successful detective might benefit from a woman in his life, an intelligent woman whose interpretation of the occasional astonishingly irrational behaviour of her sex could be relied upon.

'Your business with the lady is at an end, then?'

'Indeed, I hope so.' Faro decided he was not going to waste precious time with Alison Aird's polite interest in his investigations. 'Am I to understand that you are to be leaving us soon?'

'Yes. Mr Trelawney and the company are booked into Bournemouth for the summer season.'

Faro's heart felt unnaturally heavy as he said, 'I shall miss you.'

She smiled. 'I know.'

Did it follow that she would also miss him? He followed up his advantage. 'It seems sometimes as if I have known you for a very long time,' he said breathlessly, aware that he had said the wrong thing, for she merely inclined her head, smiled and said, 'You are very kind.'

'Will you be sorry to leave Edinburgh?'

She stared out of the window towards the Pentland Hills. 'Not really. I have been here since spring, a whole season. That is a long time for me to spend acting in the same theatre. Normally, it is two weeks and then on the road again.'

Her bleak tones aroused a dismal picture of the drudgery that lies behind those magnificent hours on stage portraying the great Shakespearean roles.

'I know so little about you,' he said helplessly, out of his depth. Where was his customary dignity? Even to his own ears, he heard the desperate note of the love-lorn who expects no mercy.

There was none. 'What is the point, when the chances are that we will never meet again?' As though conscious of her cruelty, she put out her hand and, touching his arm, said softly, 'You know enough about me, Inspector,' and, as a sop for his stricken expression, 'far more than most of the men I meet during my travels. Now, have another of Mrs Penny's scones. Of course you must, they will have been counted and she'll be mortally offended if they are not eaten. Here you are, see, I have buttered it for you.'

He groaned inwardly at this sweet domestic gesture. It struck a chord almost forgotten, for Lizzie always buttered

120

his bread. Never had he felt so alone, so in need of a woman's love and cherishing.

'Are we not even to be friends?'

'Friends? Of course we will be friends, if that will make you happy, for the short time I have left in Edinburgh.' She looked at him, head on one side, smiling, as if she could picture such an association and it pleased her. 'Yes, I would like that very much, Inspector.'

'Then may I beg that you call me by my first name?'

'Of course.' She put a hand to her mouth. 'Oh dear, I think I have forgotten what it is.'

'It's Jeremiah – my mother had a passion for biblical names, but I shortened it long ago to Jeremy.'

'Jeremy,' she repeated softly. 'I like it. It makes you sound like a little boy.'

Faro thought sourly that was not at all the impression he had hoped for, as she added, with a shake of the head, 'No more Mrs Aird – Alison, if you please. And now that we have our friendship well and truly launched, what were we talking about?'

'Your feelings about leaving Edinburgh.'

'Oh yes. Perhaps I have been too harsh in my judgement, since we have been most fortunate with our audiences. Most nights we have played to full houses. Granted the theatre is small and has many drawbacks in the way of scenery and lights, but there is something very satisfying about an enthusiastic audience. And ours, though mostly students, have been so appreciative and kind. Especially the English and Classics students. And we have even entertained classes from the senior schools – a most rewarding experience.'

'You mention students. May I then ask you something personal?'

'Of course.' But her expression was guarded.

'The very first time we met was in Greyfriars Kirkyard. You were wearing a grey cloak and a hat with a heavy grey veil, which got caught in the shrubbery.'

Her expression went completely blank, and for a heart-stopping moment Faro thought she was about to deny it. And if she had, he realised that he would have readily agreed and might even have pretended that he had been mistaken.

But at last she nodded. 'How strange. I wondered – afterwards, when we met again at the theatre – if you could possibly be my rescuer. Remember, I caught only a glimpse of your face in my involvement with my insecure bonnet.'

And the dangerous moment over, they both laughed. 'How extraordinary that we should meet again.'

Faro didn't think it in the least extraordinary, but her good-natured admission led him to ask, rather more sharply than he should, 'You knew Timothy Ferris?'

A sharp intake of breath and her eyes filled with sudden tears. 'Yes, I did. I cannot tell you – he was – he was – like the son I never had. He came to the theatre regularly and it began like so many of my young admirers. Boys who imagine they are in love with me.' She laughed. 'And I as old as their mothers, even if I can play Juliet on stage. Age seems to make no difference to their devotion.'

'"Age cannot wither her, nor custom stale her infinite variety,"' quoted Faro. 'Shakespeare could have written those words with you in mind.'

'You flatter me, but I am no Cleopatra – and I am well aware of the fact.' She sighed. 'Poor Timon. I called him that, after Timon of Athens. I liked it better than Timothy. He was so attentive, so devoted. And in the end I had to send him away.'

She was silent, and Faro saw that she was trembling. 'I little realised that I was destroying him. You know how it ended, that awful, awful death. And I was responsible— '

Sobs racked her and Faro took her in his arms, murmured the same soothing words he used to little Rose and Emily.

122

'Hush, my dear. Hush, you mustn't carry this guilt. It was not your fault that he died.'

'It was, it was.'

'It wasn't, Alison. Listen to me.' And he tilted her weeping face towards him. Gently, he put his lips to her cheek, with the bitter-sweet salt taste of her tears. As he smoothed back her hair, and she took out her handkerchief and blew her nose, he thought what a relief his next words would be to her. Maybe – maybe she would be so grateful that she might even love him a little.

'You see, Alison, we have it on very good authority that Tim Ferris wanted to marry Lily Goldie . . .'

Her eyes slid away from him. 'You mean – that girl – who died?'

'Exactly. It was because she refused him, discovered that he had been leading her on to believe he had a fortune. Then, when she learned he was penniless, she sent him packing. You see, he apparently had quite a good allowance from some benefactor or other, but when he failed his qualifying exams – so Vince tells me – this was withdrawn. He had always lived beyond his means, gambling, drinking, impressing Miss Goldie. When he knew that was all over, that's why he took his own life.'

Alison stared at him, took a deep breath and then cried out, 'Oh God, dear God. All that pain, all that agony – and no one to comfort him.'

The door opened a sliver and they both turned round.

'I thought I heard you call for more tea, Mrs Aird,' said Mrs Penny, her excuse paper-thin. Obviously she had heard the sobbing, and curiosity as to what was going on in her parlour, where her boarder was at the mercy of a gentleman caller, had overcome her.

Alison managed a bright smile and disentangled herself from Faro's arm. 'No, thank you, Mrs Penny. That was delicious.'

'Delicious,' echoed Faro.

123

Mrs Penny was reluctant to move. She frowned, looking suspiciously from one to the other.

'Mr Faro is just leaving,' said Alison, holding out her hand with a dazzling smile, calculated to convince her land-lady that nothing untoward had been happening behind that closed door. 'I will see Mr Faro out, thank you, Mrs Penny.'

At the front door, they were both silent, staring up at Arthur's Seat agleam in the afternoon sunshine.

Faro took both her hands, held them tightly. 'Just one more question, and then this painful subject will never be mentioned between us again, I promise.'

She looked at him squarely. 'If you must.'

'Did you ever meet Tim's young brother?'

'His young brother?' she repeated.

'Yes, we understand he is a boarder at St Leonard's.'

Alison thought for a moment, then shook her head. 'I didn't know that. He never mentioned a brother. But that doesn't surprise me. He took a certain pride in being an orphan.'

Mrs Penny poked her head out, her curiosity further aroused by this prolonged doorstep conversation. 'See and not get cold, Mrs Aird, dear. Remember your voice now.'

Alison gave him an impish smile and hastily released her hands, which he still held.

'May I see you again?' he whispered.

'Are you not coming to *The Merchant*? There are some free seats available and Mr Trelawney's Shylock is very credible,' she said with a mischievous glance. 'The char-acter offers such marvellous possibilities for over-acting.'

'If you are playing Portia . . .'

'I am . . .'

'Then I will come.'

Far below them, the little horse-drawn train arrived at St Leonard's Station.

'I have always promised myself to take a journey along that railway,' said Alison. 'I believe it goes to Musselburgh, and the seaside is so tempting. It is what one misses most without children. It must be years since I built a sandcastle, or dipped my toes in the ocean.'

'Then you need wait no longer. May I take you there on Sunday?'

'Oh, would you do that? Please! I shall get Mrs Penny to provide us with a picnic hamper.' And clasping her hands together like a little child, 'I shall so look forward to Sunday. Thank you – thank you, Jeremy. You have made me so happy.'

Standing on tiptoe, she kissed his cheek. And Faro walked towards Sheridan Place in a daze. Occasionally he touched the place her lips had caressed and considered himself the luckiest fellow in the whole world, from the day Alison Aird had walked into his life and he had decided to re-investigate the murder of Lily Goldie.

Content surged through him, a great wave of bliss, and he looked forward to retiring quietly to his study with its firelight glowing on his rows of books, his familiar chair and his desk. Always untidy, resisting strongly all Mrs Brook's determination to restore order, it was a lonely widower's retreat, heaven or hell, according to his mood. But it was his very own special place, where he could close the shutters against the unhappy world he inhabited by day. There he could seek refuge from his own troubles in some other time or place, in the worlds portrayed in the novels of Sir Walter Scott or Mr Charles Dickens. And there he could now weave his own dreams, more promising than any pages of a novel, about Alison Aird.

CHAPTER TWELVE

St Leonard's School was less than twenty years old, but it already smelled of boiled cabbage and wet wood, a familiar odour that Faro associated with boys' schools. It took him back to the Kirkwall of his childhood.

Everything about Headmaster Benjamin Lochhead was larger than life, from his booming voice to his flowing white beard, which instantly transformed him into an Old Testament patriarch. His parents, long dead, had shown a certain lack of insight when they chose his first name, whose initial immediately registered with several gleeful decades of boys and earned him the nickname 'Old Blockhead'. He received Faro in his lofty panelled study, an awesome place where white busts of Socrates, Homer and other scholastic worthies gazed down sternly from their high pedestals.

'Please be seated, Mr Faro. Perhaps you would like to glance over our prospectus. What age is the young gentleman?'

'Fourteen or fifteen.'

The Headmaster frowned. 'A difficult age, but one we can readily accommodate,' he added hastily.

'Headmaster, before we go any further, I must tell you that I am not Mr Faro, about to deliver a new pupil into your regime. I am Detective Inspector Faro of the Edinburgh City Police and I am here to make enquiries about a boy already with you.'

The patriarch froze, his hand in mid-air, suddenly an ungenial Santa Claus. His voice was icy. 'And what misdemeanours have my boys committed? Surely it is no serious crime which brings you to my establishment?' he added sardonically.

As Faro tried to give him a brief outline of the Gruesome Convent Murders, he found his placatory speech sounding thinner than ever.

The Headmaster made an impatient gesture. 'Yes, yes, Inspector. I have read the case.' He gave him a long glance. 'A private investigation – at the request of the unfortunate victim's relatives, you say. I do not see what my school can possibly contribute.'

'Miss Goldie was on friendly terms with Mr Timothy Ferris.'

For a moment the Headmaster frowned, and then nodded slowly. 'A former pupil of this school who took his own life. A disgraceful business. Ferris was one of our first boarders. He came to us when he was eight years old.'

This was a stroke of luck. 'And I believe Ferris Minor is a present pupil?'

'Ferris Minor?'

'Yes, his younger brother.'

'You have been misinformed, Inspector. Timothy Ferris was without relatives.'

'Are you quite certain?'

'Indeed I am.' And opening a drawer, the Headmaster handed Faro a bound volume. 'This is our register, a complete alphabetic list of our pupils for each year, back to the year eighteen-fifty when the school was opened. See for yourself if you can find a Ferris Minor.'

When Faro, after glancing through, shook his head, Lochhead continued, 'And may I ask what this Ferris Minor has done to warrant an investigation?'

'He was seen to be on friendly terms with the late Miss Goldie.'

'And where, might one ask, were these friendly terms observed?'

'At the Convent of the Sisters of St Anthony.'

Lochhead sprang to his feet, a tower of biblical wrath. 'Intolerable, intolerable. An outrageous suggestion, sir, outrageous and indecent. One of my pupils associating with a member of that establishment. I would have you know that the convent is out of bounds, strictly out of bounds. The punishment for fraternising is severe and none of my boys would risk such a thing.' Recovering from the shock, he sat down heavily and pointed a finger at the Inspector. 'Someone – someone has been leading you up the garden path, deliberately misinforming you in a desire to cast discredit upon my school. The matter, let me assure you, sir, shall not rest here,' he added severely.

Faro was aware of the danger. Should the Headmaster complain to Superintendent Mackintosh, there would be the devil to pay.

'That should not be necessary. You have my assurances, Headmaster. This is purely a private matter which will go no further than this room.'

'I am relieved to hear that.'

Faro rose to his feet. 'Perhaps before I leave, you can tell me something about Timothy Ferris.' The Headmaster made a restless movement, eager to end the interview, as Faro continued, 'May I ask in what manner his fees were paid?'

'Such matters are highly confidential, Inspector. However, in Ferris's case there was a trust fund which dealt with all financial matters.'

Faro was surprised and disappointed, remembering Vince's rumour of a rich benefactor. 'Not an individual?'

'No. It is usual in cases of orphans with well-to-do patrons, who wish to remain anonymous, to set up a trust fund.'

'I don't quite understand.'

128

The Headmaster's lip curled. 'Naturally, Inspector, if you are not a public-school man yourself. It is quite regrettable, but many pupils have, er, unfortunate backgrounds.'

'In what way?'

Lochhead sighed wearily at this lack of comprehension. 'Many are illegitimate sons of noble families, or of prosperous citizens who wish to keep such information secret for the damage it might do to their reputations – or, alas, much worse, to their business or professional life.' At that moment, Faro decided he looked almost human, as if he would have relished the sharing of a piece of gossip. Then, remembering himself in time, 'I won't delay you any further, Inspector.'

'To save embarrassment and litigation, a settlement is made through a trust fund. Yes,' said Vince that evening. 'Of course, I should have realised that. There were several cases in my own school, among the boarders.'

Lizzie had insisted that Vince be 'properly educated'. 'On account of his unfortunate background. We owe it to him, Jeremy,' she had whispered. And nothing would move her. Not even the fact that they could ill-afford fees for a private school.

Faro sighed, realising that as his heart sang with joy at the thought of Alison Aird, he was thinking less and less of Lizzie, who had been up to now the only love of his life, without once proving to be the great love he had once anticipated.

Perhaps his practical mind had been cautioned by his mother's love for his father, love doomed and yet undimmed, impervious to the ravages of time, love about which she continued to speak with such eloquence and emotion after nearly forty years. Their little cottage in Dean Village, living only for each other, the sound of his footsteps, the creaking gate, at the end of each day's labour. Safe home, another day's battle behind him, glorious as a soldier, returning to her arms again.

His violent death – his murder, she called it – cut like a knife through her world. After grief, and long before the Queen set the fashion for widows by dedicating her life as a shrine to Prince Albert, Mary Faro had been doing exactly that for her own dear Magnus for nearly forty years. The custom of Indian wives committing suttee and stoically following their husband into the funeral pyre met, not with her horror, but with her full support, as correct and fitting.

In his childhood, Faro remembered that hardly a day ever passed by without some reference to, 'Your dear father – he would have loved to see you do so-and-so, your dear father would have loved to hear you say that' – and so on.

It was his father's ghostly advice during his adulthood that was to spur him on and lead him to the Edinburgh Police Force. Mary Faro was even prepared to accept the departure of her only son to Edinburgh by consoling herself with, 'Your dear father would have been proud to see you this day.' She had refused his offer to accompany him, firmly putting behind her any idea of returning to the place of her greatest happiness and greatest sorrow.

'Besides, you will soon find a wife – and even if I wished to come with you, I have my obligations.' Her obligations were self-induced, to a tide of elderly invalids, mostly remote cousins she had made it her life's work to care for. All her pent-up maternal love had flowed into these bleak little houses on the wild shores near Kirkwall. No one in trouble or sorrow ever came to her door and left empty-handed.

'You are young and handsome, just the image of your dear father. You will soon make a life of your own – with a wife – and with grandchildren for your old mother.'

Ten years were to pass. Constable Jeremy Faro walked his Edinburgh beat, his feet well and truly on the ground, surrounded by the most sordid aspects of crime, while his head remained stubbornly in the clouds, confidently awaiting the great romance his mother had promised. It never happened. He had given up all hope of what the romantic novelettes and the great classics alike describe as falling in love, an emotion he recognised among the great writers and poets: the passions of Romeo for Juliet, of Antony for Cleopatra, both ended in tragedy. Was the reason that such ecstasy, a love one would die for, could not sustain the less rarefied atmosphere of everyday life, the drier down-to-earth elements that constituted marriage? Marriage itself, he thought, must strike the death knell of romance.

He had come to terms with what promised to be lonely bachelordom, with the bleak conclusion that there was no great love set aside for him. Then, one day, a pretty young waitress with a beguiling Highland accent was serving dinner at the hotel where he was making routine enquiries after a robbery.

Lizzie was from Skye, and prepared to be friendly to the young policeman who took her to Jenners for tea on her afternoon off. It was an occasion he found extremely pleasant, as had other occasions when he had taken other young women out to tea, or to hear a brass band. No more and no less.

After the first time, when conversation had been difficult to sustain, for they seemed to have little in common, Faro had almost decided not to see her again, but Lizzie was never good at concealing her feelings, and her look of disappointment was his undoing.

At their second meeting, she was less shy and more expansive about her early life. She and her young brother had been only a short time in Edinburgh and had not made many friends. Faro himself had made few friends since he came from Orkney. He did not consider this a disadvantage, preferring the company of books and solitary walks in the country. Colleagues in the Central Office, of his own age, touching thirty, were mostly married men with young families.

Having thought her less than twenty, he was surprised to learn that she was considerably older than her brother. Her struggles to bring up the lad, whom she was trying to educate so that he might have a better life than had been her lot, created a further bond. Her island story found a sympathetic echo in his own Orkney background.

Conscious of her own inadequacies in the matter of education and the loneliness of city life in Edinburgh, she often sought refuge in the beckoning foothills of the Pentlands. On their third meeting, she brought along her nine-year-old brother. The occasion was not a success; the boy was handsome and extremely like his sister, but he was also sullen and rebellious, ungrateful, ungracious.

Jeremy decided not to repeat the expedition, and in fact thought it as well not to continue seeing Lizzie in case his continued attentions led her to believe that he had serious intentions. The idea of a permanent relationship with the odious brother tagging along filled him with dismay.

For several weeks he returned to his solitary life, then, one day, by accident, he met her walking in Princes Street Gardens with a companion, one of the hotel maids. He found himself genuinely glad to see her again. He had missed her, and told her so. Her suddenly tear-filled eyes, her hand on his arm, beseeching, told its own story of how wounded she had been by his neglect.

Six months of 'walking-out' followed – without a single kiss, a fact which would have astonished his colleagues who from their teasing conversations imagined that the handsome, shy young constable from Orkney was 'a regular dark horse'. The pleasant undemanding relationship might have continued indefinitely had Lizzie not been dismissed by the hotel. Questioned as to why, she reluctantly admitted it was on account of a misdemeanour of her brother.

'He was very naughty and annoyed the manager. Rude to a guest, you know. He is so high-spirited, he didn't mean it.'

Faro doubted that, for although his first impression of the boy had been softened on closer acquaintance, he knew from Lizzie that his behaviour was unpredictable and he could still be a bit of a handful.

'He needs a man – a father – in his life, that's what.'

She and the boy had been asked to leave immediately. Poor Lizzie, in tears, was at her wits' end. She had nowhere to go, and although Faro realised it would hardly be considered proper or respectable to have her living in his digs, perhaps the presence of her young brother would lessen the inevitable eyebrow raising and heavy-handed teasing. His colleagues would inevitably see this step as a prelude to his forthcoming marriage.

One person was less than pleased – his young widowed landlady. Favoured with the largest servings, the best cuts of meat, even Faro guessed what were her hardly concealed designs. Of late, her overtures and hints had increased in boldness, bringing forth delighted guffaws from Faro's colleagues, and a somewhat hunted look into his own eyes.

An unpleasant week followed Lizzie's arrival: of smaller helpings, high dudgeon accompanied by door- and plate-banging from the irate landlady. The boy's behaviour was impeccable. Polite to everyone, to Faro he was friendly and helpful, even charming.

'He is so shy,' said Lizzie, 'but he does like you very much, Jeremy. Perhaps it is the uniform that made him a little nervous when you first met.'

At the end of two weeks, Faro had decided it was very pleasant to have a smiling young woman to welcome him 'home'. He was taken aback when Lizzie announced that she was leaving that weekend for Peebles.

'Why must you go to Peebles?'

'I have a situation there, in a hotel, if I want it.'

'Must you go so far away? Is there nothing suitable here in Edinburgh?'

'Nothing that keeps us here. The wage I'm being offered is far better too.' She paused uncomfortably. 'As you can guess, I have very little money left from my savings.'

Suddenly Faro's future looked very bleak. Undemanding Lizzie replaced by the triumphantly predatory landlady. The alternative was a search for new digs, much less than a convenient stone's-throw from the Central Office and most likely with less of the good food and comfort that he had grown accustomed to for the past two years.

'Lizzie,' he said, 'could I persuade you to stay – I mean, if we married?'

She looked at him and her eyes filled with tears. 'Of course I would stay then. Jeremy Faro, are you seriously asking me to marry you?'

'Yes, yes. I'd like that – very much. More than anything.'

Conscious that he was making an idiot of himself with his first ever proposal, he leaned over to kiss her and was surprised by the warmth of her reaction, by her soft and loving arms tight about his neck as she whispered, 'Oh, my dear, I have loved you for such a long time.'

It was then he realised he had said nothing about love, that love in fact had never entered his head. He patted her shoulder, and clearing his throat stammered out, 'There, there – I love you.'

The effect of his declaration was to have Lizzie burst into tears, cast him aside and sit down at the table, beating her arms upon it like one demented. Her attitude of unutterable despair took Faro by surprise. It was not at all what he had been led to believe might be the reaction to his proposal and Lizzie's acceptance.

When he tried to comfort her, she clung to him, rained passionate kisses upon him and then again thrust him aside.

'No. No, dear. It can never be. I was foolish to think you could love me.'

'But I do. Haven't I said so?'

There were more sobs. 'Do not make it more difficult for me, I beg you. I should never have given way, encouraged you to propose. Before you begin to hate me, you must believe that I love you with all my heart. I shall never, never love anyone else. I'll love you and only you until I die. But I can never, never marry you.'

'What are you talking about? You love me and yet you say we can't be married. Why on earth not?' And then the thought struck him. 'Is it the boy? Is that it? Does your brother dislike me so much? Tell me, don't be afraid. Is that it?'

'If only it was that simple,' she whispered.

'It doesn't sound very simple to me. It is the boy, isn't it?'

'It is, Jeremy. But the boy is not what you think.' She clutched his hand so tightly that it hurt. 'You see, he isn't my brother.' And in a whisper, 'He's my son. My bastard son.'

Faro stared at her. 'But he couldn't be – you couldn't . . .'

'Oh yes. He is, and I could – and did. I was fifteen – taken, by force – it was one of the laird's house-guests up for the shooting. You could never want to marry me now. No decent man would want marriage with such a degraded, wicked woman as me,' she sobbed.

'You're wrong, Lizzie, you're wrong about that. I could – and will marry you. And I'll be a father to the boy. The past is gone and we can't change that. It is the future that's our concern – our future together. So now we'll never talk about this again – do you hear? Never.'

Jeremy Faro was good to his word. A good husband to Lizzie and a good father to Vince, who soon became the very apple of his eye. Lizzie was a good wife, although he had to admit that their marriage didn't exalt his senses, nor could he by any feat of the imagination mistake it for the love that he had read about in books. He was not complaining, he was content with Lizzie, shrewdly guessing

135

that in every relationship no two people love to the same measure. There is one who kisses and one who is kissed, one who gives and one who takes.

Lizzie never wavered in her love for him, and his mother, watching them, remembered that it was like seeing her own love for his dear father relived and advised her son, very sternly, 'Never has any woman loved a man as much as that lass loves you, except for the Queen and myself, that is. Treasure it, lad. It's more precious than gold.'

Faro had thought that marriage would last until they were both old people sitting by the fireside together. It had not dawned upon him that his strong healthy Lizzie, who had given birth to two daughters with a minimum of trouble, would give her own life in bearing him a son.

Stricken to the heart, after he laid her in the grave, he decided there would be no more loving for him. He would not ask fate for miracles. He would count himself fortunate to have Rose and Emily, who adored him, and Vince whom he was proud to call his son. He was clever, and the private school had a bursary system, and that, added to Faro's own promotion, saw him through university.

Faro considered that he had been amply repaid for those early sacrifices. In two days' time, Vince would celebrate his twenty-second birthday.

'How shall we celebrate?' he asked.

'Dear Mrs Brook would love to have a tea party,' said Vince. 'She is longing to put on display a full account of her culinary genius.'

'That's a splendid idea.'

'I thought we might ask Rob and Walter, of course, and Hugo.'

'A bachelor tea party?'

Vince grinned. 'You look quite disappointed, Stepfather. Actually I thought you might like to invite Mrs Aird to bring along some young ladies from the theatre. Saturday is a convenient time, before the evening performance, which begins an hour later than normal to allow the cast to recover from the matinée performance. Afterwards, I thought we might go and see Mrs Aird as Cleopatra and then supper at one of our old student haunts.' He laughed. 'No, Stepfather, I don't mean "The Gay Japanee" – somewhere much more in keeping with your respectable image.'

Faro smiled wryly. On two occasions he had been present when the police had searched the notorious Leith Walk howff, a hostelry which was a thinly disguised brothel, beloved of the student population, and especially of those sons of respectable houses who of necessity had to sow their wild oats before settling down to honourable Edinburgh professions in church, state and law.

'I'll write the invitations, if you wish. And now, Stepfather, back to the business of our second murderer.' Drawing up a sheet of paper he began to write.

'I've made a list already, lad.'

'I know, I've seen it. But do bear with me. After all, no two people viewing the same events see them in quite the same fashion. And that is perhaps – that tiny island of discrepancy – where we might indeed find the clue to his identity.'

Faro approved of such thoroughness. 'Very well. Back to the beginning. First of all, we have Hymes.'

'Hymes,' wrote Vince, 'who we have agreed is unlikely to be the murderer of Lily Goldie, on the evidence of the Mother Superior, of Maureen Hymes, and our own conclusions.'

'Which are?'

'That he would have strangled her with his hands, not tied a scarf about her neck afterwards, as I am convinced, from the post-mortem, was what actually happened.'

'If she had been the first victim instead of the second, then Hymes might have murdered her, in mistake for his wife.'

'Provided that the early morning light was dim enough and he came upon her from behind.'

'All fairly thin, rather too many suppositions,' said Faro.

'Right. Tim Ferris?' wrote Vince whose reaction had been, 'I told you so, didn't I?' when Faro had reported his conversation with Mrs Aird.

'Highly probable. If he had been alive at the time of Lily Goldie's murder, he would have been the obvious suspect.'

'Indeed he would. He would have had to produce some very good evidence as to his whereabouts at the time.'

'Very difficult when at six o'clock in the morning, when Lily Goldie took her walk up to Salisbury Crags, he and a large proportion of middle-class Edinburgh were still abed.'

'Talking about Ferris, what about the mysterious missing younger brother? Remember it was Lily Goldie who introduced him to Miss Burnleigh as Ferris's brother,' said Vince.

'Yet Ferris never mentioned his existence to Alison Aird, who one imagines he would confide in.'

'Ferris Minor seems to have been a figment of Lily's imagination. I wonder what her reasons were. Why did she lie about it?'

'That is something we will never know, lad. Some woman's wiles.'

Vince nodded. 'And we gather she had plenty of them. Liked teasing and goading other females.' He thought for a moment. 'What about Clara Burnleigh, anyway?'

'Her reasons for disappearing from the convent and giving a false address seem genuine enough. There certainly was this very nasty scandal in her family, and she's very intent upon climbing up the social ladder – and not very bright, I suspect – besides, what was her motive? Lily Goldie wasn't any threat to her. What about your Miss McDermot?'

'We know she left before the murder took place.' Vince smiled. 'I would be prepared to vouch for her. If only you had met her . . .' he added with a sigh. So that leaves us with the Mad Bart. By the process of elimination, Stepfather, I can't help thinking he is most likely to be our man. Consider the condition of his hands. That he might have been incapable of exerting the pressure needed for strangulation and therefore, when he pushed her off, he went down to make sure she was dead. Instead, he found her still alive and tied the scarf about her neck.'

'There's one thing you haven't considered. How did the old man get up Salisbury Crags? It's a stiffish climb for an old man with rheumatism in his knees.' Faro shook his head. 'I must confess that is the one improbability in your hypothesis.'

'We've never worked out how the murderer lured her up there in the early morning in the first place, Stepfather. There must have been some irresistible reason, since *rigor mortis* had not set in when she was discovered. When she got to the mortuary she hadn't been dead more than a couple of hours.' Vince threw down his pen.

'Well, it has to be one of them,' said Faro. 'Or else a complete stranger.'

'A passer-by filled with a mad impulse at the sight of an attractive young woman walking in a lonely place is usually a rapist. And we know she wasn't sexually assaulted.'

'Whoever murdered Lily Goldie had a very good reason, lad.'

'And knew about Hymes murdering his wife and took a chance on him being blamed for both.'

Faro shook his head. 'I have a feeling that we've taken a wrong turning somewhere, lad. That the answer is staring us in the face and we're just not seeing it.' He paused before adding, 'There is one other person who could have murdered Lily Goldie and might have had excellent reasons for doing so.'

'You mean – the Reverend Mother?' Vince sounded doubtful.

Faro laughed. 'Seriously?'

'Yes, if she is a religious fanatic, felt that the presence of Sarah Hymes and Lily Goldie had besmirched her reputation.'

'Then she would be insane.'

Vince nodded solemnly and Faro said, 'A mad baronet and a mad Mother Superior?'

'It isn't beyond the bounds of possibility. Or it might have been a fanatical nun who worshipped the Mother Superior and hated Lily Goldie.'

Faro filled his pipe and lit it thoughtfully. 'In my experience, Vince lad, very few murders are planned and executed by madmen or women . . .'

'. . . with the exception of the *crime passionnel*.'

'I grant you that. But the murder we are dealing with has all the indications of having been thought out very carefully by someone of exceptional intelligence.' Watching the smoke spiralling, he said, 'There is one other person.'

As Vince consulted his list again, Faro said, 'McQuinn.'

'Now you can't be serious.'

'Oh yes, I can. Consider him for a moment. He has access to the convent, he is friendly with the teachers, sweet on Lily, according to the maids. Think, lad, there are infinite possibilities.'

'You mean she might have spurned his advances? I thought he had rather a lot of lady-friends and one more or less would have made little difference.'

'But what if Lily was the one he really wanted?'

'There's only one flaw, I can see. If he had wanted it to look like Hymes's work, then being a policeman, he would have made a more convincing job of her murder. He would have strangled her, exactly as Hymes did Sarah, left bruising marks on her throat. He would never have thrown her down and tied that scarf around her neck afterwards.'

140

When Faro was silent, he added, 'I know you don't like the pompous McQuinn, but you must not let your personal prejudice influence you. After all, this is a murder case.'

Vince succeeded in sounding so like Superintendent Mackintosh that Faro laughed out loud at the apparent absurdity of his hypothesis. But not for long.

CHAPTER THIRTEEN

The next two days at the Central Office were very trying indeed, thanks to McQuinn, whose recent performance seemed to have impressed his superiors so greatly that the Constable had now been allocated as special assistant to Detective Inspector Faro.

Remembering his own early days, Faro knew what that meant. Promotion was on the way. McQuinn had but to prove himself and if he, Faro, didn't watch out, they would be saying he was too old for the job.

McQuinn was clearly bursting with pride and new importance, thought Faro with disgust, watching his over-eager smile charm old ladies, as did his offer of a helping hand. Faro had observed all too often in the Princes Street Gardens evidence of McQuinn's pouter pigeon breadth of chest charming their daughters, especially when accompanied by some outrageous piece of gallantry.

Normally a fair-minded man who scorned prejudices in others, Faro had to admit that the constable showed the makings of a good detective. If only his presence and his patronising manner were less obnoxious, especially when he seized every opportunity of demolishing Faro's long-standing theories with a sneer.

The fact that McQuinn had found a speedy solution to a recent case of embezzlement and a daring jewel theft was even more galling. He could also move with amazing rapidity and, taking off after the thief, vaulted fences and low walls like a race-horse, leaving Faro winded, staring bleakly after him.

Returning triumphant with Black Tam's nephew, railing down curses and promises of his uncle's vengeance, McQuinn found a grim-faced Faro ready with the cuffs. 'Allow me, Inspector, this is my man.' And later, adding insult to his superior officer's injury, 'I'm filling in my report, Inspector, and I'm saying that "we" apprehended him. I hope you approve.' When Faro growled that it wasn't strictly true, McQuinn continued amiably, 'I'm prepared to concede the point. After all, this kind of work, it's really a young man's job. You have to be fit.'

'Damn your impudence,' said Faro, and, snatching the pen, he crossed out 'we' and substituted 'PC McQuinn'. 'I'll have you know I'm not decrepit yet – not by a long way.'

'To be sure you're not, Inspector. Just a wee bit out of condition. Let's face it, this happens, so I'm told, to every man with advancing age.'

Such remarks succeeded in making him feel like a doddering ancient, and it was as well for McQuinn that the Superintendent entered the office at that moment, or the Constable might have received severe chastisement from Faro in the form of a punch on the nose.

On his way home, Faro called in at the Pleasance Theatre to leave the invitations for Vince's party. In the corridor he met a black-clad figure almost unrecognisable as Alison, hurrying into her dressing-room to change out of her Portia costume. Peering round the door at him, she snatched the envelope.

'Forgive me, Jeremy. I cannot talk to you just now. I have an important dinner engagement in the New Town and I'm late already. Do forgive me,' she repeated, and closed the door firmly.

Hugo Rich, however, was disposed to conversation, displaying an almost schoolboyish relish in criminal investigation, the disposal of corpses and other ghoulish matters.

Faro finally made his escape, and neither his opinion of McQuinn nor his temper was improved when he discovered the Constable handing Alison into a brougham waiting outside. As the Constable leaned in her direction, with his jaunty confidential manner, that mobile handsome face staring down into hers, peals of laughter reached Faro. Light-hearted as she never is with me, he thought disgustedly. Too much in a hurry to exchange half a dozen words with me, but with all the time in the world for McQuinn.

The sight stirred him to unexpected fury, especially as, at his approach, they both turned, their faces wiped clean of expression, leaving him to wonder suspiciously whether he had been the object of their merriment. And the thought that he had been made to appear ridiculous in Alison's eyes smote him to the heart.

Danny McQuinn and Alison Aird so occupied his thoughts on the way to Sheridan Place that he realised his interest in the case of Lily Goldie was dwindling rapidly. There were too many paths that led nowhere and he realised that if he was to be absolutely honest with himself it was not Hymes, nor his sister, nor even Lily Goldie, that had made him take on this private investigation.

As he opened the front gate, he realised he was never going to solve this mystery, or the identity of the second murderer – if such existed – if he let himself be diverted by destructive emotions of jealousy. Indeed, when he examined his own motives, he saw that personal pride and vindication were both involved. That he might prove to Central Office that they had bungled and that he was indispensable. There was even a small unworthy hope that he might find something to discredit Constable McQuinn and dash that supercilious smile from his face for ever.

Even Vince's original enthusiasm was daunted, and he must give up soon. In a few weeks, he would have served his *locum tenens* with Dr Kellar. Then he would be setting

144

up his own surgery in the house. For his future as a fully fledged medical practitioner, Faro had installed on the front door an elegant brass plate.

Faro waited by the drawing-room window for Vince's return from Dr Kellar's and dashed downstairs in time to witness his surprise and delight at this unexpected present.

'Doctor Vincent Beaumarcher Laurie,' he exclaimed proudly, and, eyeing it critically, 'Do you think the letters are large enough, Stepfather?' He breathed on an imaginary speck of dust, which he polished with his sleeve.

'Big enough, I hope, to bring a small army of Newington and Grange folk trooping up to your door as patients,' said Faro, standing back for a last look before following him inside.

'But only for a while, Stepfather. You know I intend to become Queen's Surgeon, once I have enough money – nothing less will satisfy,' said Vince solemnly.

'Not even being a good doctor and saving lives?'

'There's nothing very distinguished in attending to broken heads and bones, to coughs and sneezes and bringing babies into the world.'

'A lot of doctors spend their whole lives doing it, lad, and consider that reward enough.'

Vince banged his fist on the table. 'Oh no, Stepfather, not for me. These doctors you speak of with their fine surgeries in the New Town, they have mostly come from respectable middle-class homes. They're not like me – I'm different – you're not forgetting that, are you? I'm only the bastard son of a servant girl,' he added bitterly.

Faro winced at the words and Vince smiled. 'Oh, that still hurts, doesn't it? That you weren't the first, that my mother had a child before she married you.'

'I never gave it a thought. I loved you, little devil that you were, from almost the first moment we met . . .'

'And I hated you,' said Vince slowly, 'for stealing my

145

mother, the only person in the world who belonged to me absolutely, the only person I would ever have who was flesh of my flesh, bone of my bone. And now she's gone too.'

This tirade was no new experience for Faro. He knew that Vince thought of Lizzie acutely each time his birthday came round, remembering the pain and shame in which she had brought him into the world. He put his hand on the boy's shoulder.

'You still have me, lad, and you've been more to me than many a son to his father. I've been so proud of you.'

As they waited for the first guests to arrive, Mrs Brook having set a table that was a masterpiece of culinary art, Vince looked out of the window at the afternoon sun gleaming on the Pentland Hills and sighed.

'If only mother could be with us today,' and, turning to Faro, he asked bitterly, 'Why did she have to die, anyway? So unnecessary.'

'That's one of the things you might discover in your life as a family doctor – just why so many women bear children and then both die within days . . .'

They were both silent, in attitudes of grief, as if Lizzie had died just days ago. She seemed to be there in the room with them, with her sweet voice and gentle laughter.

They both started as the door opened to admit the party guests, led by Alison Aird, holding a cake with candles already lit, and followed by Hugo, Rob, Walter and a trio of young gentlemen from medieval Venice.

'Happy birthday to you – happy birthday, dear Vince,' they sang, and everyone applauded. Then, bowing, they swept off their caps, to be revealed as the young actresses still in their *Merchant* costumes.

'Vince, you awful creature, Hugo assured us that it was to be fancy dress.'

146

Vince laughed, rolling his eyes wickedly. 'Fellow couldn't miss the chance to glimpse such fine limbs.'

'You would not have said that if you had seen us wandering along the Pleasance,' said Beth.

'Nonsense,' said Hugo. 'Passers-by were quite unmoved by the sight, as if medieval players were a regular occurrence in Newington.'

'Not even ones with such unmanly curves?' said Vince. 'And why aren't you in fancy dress, Mrs Aird? Having seen your Portia, I'd say you make an admirable Venetian gentleman.'

'We tried to persuade her. She has the perfect figure,' said Marie with an envious sigh. 'Beautiful long slender legs.'

'Ladies, ladies, please,' said Alison, 'spare my blushes.' She looked round, appealing. 'They do exaggerate, you know. Only the very young actresses like themselves can play convincing boys.'

'And the other way round,' said Hugo. 'Boys will be girls, since Shakespeare did not have the original commodity to chose from.'

'No doubt that is why his more mature ladies, like Lady Macbeth and Cleopatra, must have been extremely trying for a youth to play with conviction,' said Vince.

'"Antony shall be brought drunken forth,"' quoted Hugo in profound tones. Everyone cheered as he added in sepulchral aside to an imaginary audience, 'As he is regularly at the end of each performance.' He pointed dramatically at Alison to complete the quotation. When she declined, he continued, '"And I shall see some squeaking Cleopatra boy my greatness, I' the posture of a whore."'

The actresses groaned. 'Do give over, Hugo dear, we're not working now,' said Beth. 'There's a good fellow,' she added with an affectionate peck at his cheek, which received an appreciative embrace and some applause. The two, in Vince's parlance, were 'very smitten'.

147

There were cheers as Mrs Brook brought in the tea tray, and everyone sat down at the table to enjoy her hot buttered scones.

'We were very impressed with your brass plate,' said Marie shyly. 'Beaumarcher – that's an unusual name. Are you related to the famous earls?'

Vince had arrived home a little drunk from a celebratory drink with his medical friends, otherwise he would not have abandoned his normal discretion and waxed eloquent upon his bastardy and upon the identity of the rich man who had fathered him.

'The gratification of a few minutes of lust. A few minutes . . . that's all it takes, to father a child. Did you know that, Mrs Aird?' he asked Alison who sat on his other side.

Across the table, Faro was aware that her happy smile had been replaced by a haunted look.

'Vince, lad – really,' he said. 'Ladies present.'

Alison recovered and gave him a bright smile. Faro realised that if Vince had hoped to shock her, he was in for a disappointment.

She laughed. 'My dear Vince, I have always considered the father's role in procreation somewhat minor, and that it didn't seem quite fair, despite what the Bible says on the subject, that women should bear all the shame but are not supposed to have any of the pleasure.' She added, with surprising frankness, 'And I doubt whether even the cleverest of doctors will be able to change the laws of biology.'

But Vince didn't hear. He had extracted a rosebud from Mrs Brook's arrangement and was endeavouring to attach it to Marie's tunic, an effort requiring considerable assistance from that young lady, who was enjoying every moment.

Alison watched with amusement and swept aside Faro's whispered apologies. 'The young like to feel outrageous on occasions, and what better time than on a birthday, the beginning of a new year?'

'I assure you, he doesn't usually behave so abominably.'

'Perhaps something else upset him,' she said anxiously. 'Whatever it was, I freely forgive him.'

The lad has everything, thought Faro, looks, brains and yet he cannot forget, will never forget, that his birth puts him beyond the pale of polite society. And sometimes Faro took a good hard look at that same Edinburgh society and the seething hypocrisy of its professional and middle classes, that Vince wished to emulate. The respectability that was paper thin and, once scratched, revealed horrors of child abuse, incest, sodomy – a whole world of crawling nastiness that erupted into occasional scandals, quickly suppressed by a handshake containing a large sum of money. Scandals which not even the most forthright editor would allow to be exposed in his newspaper.

'Yes, do let's go there . . .'

'Everyone – listen . . .'

'A picnic tomorrow – over on the Fife coast.'

'We take the ferry, it's only half a mile from the landing stage.'

'What a splendid idea.'

'You must come too, Stepfather.'

Faro looked at Alison, who clapped her hands delightedly. 'Yes, Jeremy, of course you must come with us.'

Faro allowed himself to be persuaded but he was bitterly disappointed. He had been looking forward to taking Alison to Musselburgh on the horse-drawn railway, to having a day alone with her. She had clearly forgotten all about their arrangement and now, apparently, if he was to enjoy her company at all, it must be within the group of Vince's young friends.

The picnic spot had been suggested by Vince. He was to be the leader. Mrs Brook was prevailed upon to pack up the remnants of the birthday feast and wine, which pleased her since the tea table groaned with enough food to feed a regiment.

It was a merry party who dispersed for the theatre in gleeful anticipation that the perfect weather Edinburgh was at present enjoying would hold for a few days longer.

When at last Faro and Vince took their seats in the Pleasance Theatre, the curtain rose on *Antony and Cleopatra*. Faro had only seen Alison thus far in *Othello*, and here was a vastly different portrayal. Unbelievable, he thought, watching the exquisite, irresistible Queen of the Nile, whose beauty turned men to clay in her small hands and 'kiss'd away kingdoms and provinces'. That 'a lass unparallel'd' could on a different night be the simple, innocent, hero-worshipping Desdemona.

Even Topaz Trelawney's Antony was a mercifully subdued performance, although his 'I am dying, Egypt, dying' raised a misguided cheer from a rowdy element in the audience. When Cleopatra died with the asp at her breast, the scene was so heart-stopping, and Faro was so absorbed into believing what he saw, that he felt the curtain should rise on her lifeless form. That was how she should be remembered, not smiling hand-in-hand with a posturing Antony to a tumultuous, ear-splitting ovation.

He felt dazed as they left the theatre, it having been decided that everyone needed to retire early in order to catch the early morning ferry across to Fife, carriages having been arranged to transport them to Queensferry.

Vince declined the invitation to accompany Rob and Walter to Rutherford's and walked rather sharply in the direction of Sheridan Place.

'I've had enough birthday celebrations for one year,' he said in answer to Faro's question. 'And I have an infernal toothache – all those iced cakes. A hot toddy and I think I'll turn in. Of course – I'll be right as rain in the morning.'

When morning came, Vince looked round the door, weary and heavy-eyed. 'Been up all night with this damnable tooth. I think it's abscessed. I feel like death, and a picnic would be the final straw. Be a good soul, Stepfather, give them my apologies. Of course you must go. Everyone is depending on it.' And without further comment, he retreated once more into his darkened bedroom.

Groans of disappointment greeted Vince's non-arrival, and Marie looked particularly sad. An hour later, however, the party had regained their cheerful anticipation and were stepping down from the ferry after a remarkably smooth and pleasant crossing of the River Forth.

A pretty wooded dell was their destination.

'It's the perfect picnic spot for a perfect summer day,' said Faro, who had been appointed their leader, as the little group followed him triumphant through summer sounds of insects busy with their hidden world, to a chorus of seabirds, and larks rising high in the swaying long grass.

As they spread out the cloth on the grass, they found their activities keenly observed by timid rabbits, and even a shy squirrel put in an appearance. Rob had brought his flute along and there was a great deal of merriment, which irritated Faro, as the sun heralded time's passing and he realised that he was to have no time alone with Alison. No time, and so much he wanted to tell her.

At last Hugo intoned in his best Shakespearean imitation of Topaz Trelawney, 'Enough, good Sir Rob. Put aside merriment, forsooth. "Music, moody food, Of us that trade in love." Come, my sweeting,' and taking Beth's hand, they raced towards the wood, their laughter echoing back to the group of friends. Soon other couples had similar ideas, and Marie too found herself a Sunday-afternoon suitor.

To his considerable joy and relief, Faro saw that he and Alison, busily gathering up the remnants of the picnic, were alone. At last she leaned against the mossy bank, hands behind her head, staring up at the sky.

'Isn't it beautiful?' she said. 'So warm, so peaceful. A truly perfect summer's day. Just look at that sky.'

Faro had removed his jacket, rolled back his shirt-sleeves, and lay back beside her, their bare arms touching.

'"Sometimes we see a cloud that dragonish; a vapour sometimes like a bear or lion, a tower'd citadel . . ." What's
next?'

'"A pendent rock, A forked mountain, or blue prom-
ontory, With trees upon't,"' Alison supplied softly. 'What
is it you see, Jeremy?'

Faro looked down at her. 'You. Only you, my dear.'
And leaning over, he kissed her gently on the lips.

'Idiot,' but she was smiling and she made no resistance.
'Dear idiot.'

'I grant you that. I think I am idiotically, wildly in love
with you. What have you to say to that on your perfect
summer's day?' And kneeling, he began to gather her into
his arms.

This time there was no gentle response, no acquies-
cence. She sprang away from him, her eyes searching. 'No,
no— '

'Don't concern yourself about our young friends,' he
whispered, 'I hardly imagine they have disappeared to
gather wildflowers.'

'No, Jeremy. No, I say.' She evaded his hands and sat bolt
upright. 'I am not concerned with our young friends, only
with you. I absolutely forbid you to fall in love with me.'

'You cannot do that – you are too late.'

'I am not too late to discourage you.' Her eyes, regarding
him, were tragic, haunted. 'Be my friend, be anything, but
do not seek to be my lover – I implore you.'

'What if I don't wish any of those roles, but something
much more permanent in your life?'

For a moment as she looked at him, her eyes filled with
tears. 'You dear, dear man. Have you seriously considered
what you are suggesting? Not even you, I am sure, can
imagine me in the role of a policeman's wife.' Her laugh
was harsh. 'Oh my dear, it is too preposterous for words.'
And, seeing his expression, she touched his arm gently.
'Jeremy, don't let me hurt you – I don't want that. I am

152

leaving Edinburgh soon and our paths are unlikely ever to cross again.'

'Unless we want them to . . .'

She nodded. 'Oh yes, then the world would not be too wide to hold us apart. But you see, I don't love you . . .'

'You might, given time,' he said desperately, conscious that he had lost her already.

'That is not the way it happens – not for me. I have loved only twice in my whole life and I now know with certainty that it is a process I will never – no, I can never – repeat.' She looked at him. 'But had we two met – in some other circumstances – I think I might have loved you.'

'Hello there – hello?' The echoing calls from the wood announced the return of those other lovers, many with flushed countenances and a certain amount of disarray which announced that they had been more successful in their wooing than Faro.

The ferry's arrival was delayed by engine trouble, difficult to set right on a Sunday, and there was a considerable delay before they restarted. The boatman who made the announcement added, 'I hope ye all have warm clothes,' and pointing up at the sky, 'See those clouds gathering? Weather's changing. See how the water's ruffled? We're in for a bad spell, mark my words. We'll have storms before nightfall.'

The picnic party accepted this setback to their day with good-natured resilience and decided that they might as well consume the rest of the food and indulge in songs and music, accompanied by Rob's flute, until the repairs were carried out.

It was dark and the rain was falling steadily when at last the ferry limped into Queensferry again. Once again the engine failed, half-way across the river, and had to wait for tugs to pull it into the little harbour.

Alison had said little. Like everyone else she seemed tired, irritated by the long delays. Faro offered to see her

153

to Mrs Penny's and was surprised when she accepted.

'I have some magical drops for the toothache, given to me years ago by an old African chief. All the cast swear by them. I'm sorry I cannot let you borrow them. Often at night, a persistently nagging tooth keeps me sleepless. I am too much of a coward to have it removed, so I always have the drops by me. But I'd be happy to come back with you, and administer a dose to poor Vince.'

They arrived in Sheridan Place in a heavy downpour, and all Faro's thoughts about Alison and her obstinate refusal to fall in love with him were completely obliterated by the scene that was awaiting them.

CHAPTER FOURTEEN

Faro let himself in and, directing Alison up to the drawing-room, went in search of Vince. He found him in Mrs Brook's basement kitchen, her normally pristine well-scrubbed table festooned with bloodied linen. His clothes torn, head and hand bandaged, Vince was leaning back in a chair while Mrs Brook attended to his broken face.

Mrs Brook turned to Faro, very near to tears. 'Here's a terrible thing, Inspector. Poor lad here, near murdered. Set upon coming home, he was.'

Faro looked down at him. Where was beauty now? Vince's eyes were swollen, half-closed, his lips bleeding. He looked barely conscious. Faro took his hand, bleeding and bruised, nails broken.

'Vince, lad?'

Vince opened his eyes with difficulty. 'Hello, Stepfather.'

'Who did this to you?'

'Keelies.'

Mrs Brook hovered. 'If you think this is bad, Inspector, you should have seen him when that nice polis, McQuinn, carried him home. I hardly recognised him, covered in blood he was, the poor lamb.'

'McQuinn, you say?'

'Gone now. If it hadn't been for him, I would have been killed. God, I can never thank him enough. Saved my life. That's fine, Mrs Brook. Fine now.' He struggled to his feet. 'Thank you – no more. No bones broken, thank God . . .'

'. . . for small mercies,' added Mrs Brook. 'Such wickedness in a nice respectable neighbourhood. I don't know what this world is coming to, that I don't.'

'Let's go upstairs, Stepfather. All right now. I can manage.'

Faro settled him in the armchair and poured out a large glass from the decanter on the table.

'Thanks, Stepfather. I'll try not to spill your best brandy.' He drank it at a gulp. 'Sorry not to savour it in the proper fashion – that's better.'

'I think we'll consider this medicinal. Here, have another.' Watching him sip slowly and painfully this time, Faro asked, 'Now, what happened?'

'I'm glad to see you again. Did you have a splendid time in Fife?'

'Yes, Mrs Aird's upstairs. With something for your toothache.'

'Toothache – God, I need more than that. What a kindly thought – I'm grateful . . .'

'Vince – for God's sake – I'm waiting to be told what happened to you.'

'My infernal toothache got worse. Went to see Doctor Kellar and, much against his will, it being the Sabbath and so forth, he extracted it. God, that was agony. I felt even worse, groggy, wretched.' He looked at Faro doubtfully, then said, 'I have these friends who open the backdoor of their howff on Sundays – just for a few friends . . .'

'Strictly illegal – I don't think I should know about that.'

'Illegal or not, it saved my sanity. I'll spare you the details, but I left rather late and, feeling much improved, called in at Mrs Penny's to make my excuses to the divine Marie – and found that none of you had returned. I didn't attach a great deal of importance to that, but decided, as the effects of many restorative drams were wearing off, that I'd better make my way home. Took the short cut, down Gibbet Lane.'

156

'Which you should know is notorious for lurking footpads after dark. You were taking a chance – all the scum from the Warrens at Wormwoodhall gather there, hoping for a kill.'

'Which they damned near got!' He sighed. 'I was tired, drunk too, I must admit. Makes one reckless. Anyway – keelies set on me. If it hadn't been for McQuinn appearing when I was still able to yell for help, I'd be dead.'

'I'll get his report at the office. I presume he set off in hot pursuit immediately after bringing you home.'

'I rather think not.'

'He damned well should have done. That's the rule. Quickly attend the victim, then pursue the attacker. He'll have the Superintendent to answer, if he hasn't reported in immediately.'

'Because the victim is your stepson?' Vince smiled through swollen lips. 'All I lost besides my pride was my purse and a shilling – not much in it after a night's illegal drinking.' He paused, and with a shrewd glance at Faro, said, 'You'd like to get McQuinn on this, wouldn't you?'

'That's beside the point. He knows the procedure.'

'In this instance, if he hasn't done his duty, it is because I asked him not to.'

'You – what? After what they did to you?'

'That's right. You see, I'm not the only one they're after. I was just the beginning – it's you next – and maybe Mrs Aird.'

'Mrs Aird?'

'Thought that would bring you up sharp in your tracks. Ouch. God, I shouldn't laugh, hurts like hell.'

'Vince, what's this about Mrs Aird?'

'I'd better tell you the whole story.'

'Yes – and if you can bear it, start at the beginning – and I want all the details.'

'When they jumped me, I didn't stand a cat in hell's chance. Even if I hadn't been a bit unsteady with the drink, I couldn't have fought them off. Anyway, when the beg fellow held me and rifled my pockets, I thought that was all they wanted. The next thing . . .' He stopped and took a quick drink, '. . . the next thing, they had me down on the ground, kicking at me everywhere with their great boots. I thought I was a goner and that their leader – a great brute of a fellow – was going to use his boot to kick my face in, when suddenly he sat me up, took hold of my coat lapels.'

'This big fellow – what was he like?'

'It was pretty dark, but he was built like a barn door. Black hair, beard— '

'Black Tam o' Leith,' said Faro. 'He and his lads have been on our books for a long while. Robbery with violence. We got his nephew behind bars last week.'

'In my case I suspect they were more interested in the violence. This black devil's foul breath was on my face and he said, "I'll let you go this time, Doctor Laurie." '

'Doctor Laurie – so he knew who you were?'

Vince nodded. 'Oh yes, he knew. "If we went any further, it would be murder, ye ken that, laddie. That we could destroy you, finish you off. That would give my lads the greatest pleasure. But what we've done to you is just to show your stepfather a bit of what might happen to someone like himself and that fancy actress of his – her that goes to the Quaker Mission. Tell him to leave me and mine in peace – or else!" '

'The Quaker Mission? I suppose the children told him.' Alison had come in quietly and was leaning against the door, her face pale with shock.

'Or had it beaten out of them, more likely,' said Faro.

'Oh, Vince, my dear.' Alison ran across and, kneeling by his side, took his hands, stroked back his hair, murmured soothing words. It was a scene unexpectedly maternal which smote Faro's heart with love renewed.

Vince was holding out his glass. 'Yes, please, I'd love another drink.'

Alison glanced quickly at Faro before going to the table with its decanters and water carafe.

'I'm used to being threatened,' said Faro. 'Think nothing about it, a hazard of the job. But to use my family . . .'

Alison was again kneeling by Vince's side. 'Drink this.'

'Ugh – what's this? Water?'

'Yes, my dear. And you're going to have a good sleep, which is what you need most. It's only laudanum.'

A sudden growl of thunder shook the room, followed by the angry hiss of rain, like the arrows of an army in search of the three frightened people beleaguered, crouching, behind the room's closed shutters.

Alison shivered. 'I have a request. May I stay here for the night? I am – I am so afraid to go home. I know I shall never sleep, and besides I might be of more use where I can look after him.'

'Mrs Brook can do that – besides we have no spare bedroom prepared . . .'

'You have several comfortable sofas – a rug is all I need.' And looking into Faro's stern face with tragic haunted eyes, she whispered, 'I beg you, let me stay. I had a son once.'

Faro slept little that night. Occasionally he awoke to hear a creaking board or movements in the kitchen below, a tap turned on. Once he went downstairs and found Alison making tea.

'What time is it?'

'Dawn,' she said. 'Listen to the birds. The storm is over, all is well with the world again.'

'Vince?'

'I have kept my vigil. He is sleeping soundly. Now have some tea, it will refresh you. No?' She put a hand on his arm. 'And do not look so worried, Jeremy. Go back to sleep!' And, standing on tiptoe, she kissed him lightly on the cheek.

'I won't sleep . . .'

'Would you like some of my magic drops?'

He looked at her, conscious that his heart was in his eyes and that the most magical of all would be to make love to her against that dawn chorus. Afterwards, how he would sleep!

When he came downstairs again at eight o'clock, she had gone and Vince was in the breakfast room. In bright sunlight, his broken face looked even worse than by lamplight.

Faro groaned. 'As Christ is my witness, I'll get Big Tam for this – if it's the last thing I do . . .'

'Careful, Stepfather – it might be just that.'

'Look, lad, this is a situation I'm used to. There are always petty criminals out for my blood, and I wouldn't have thought Black Tam had enough imagination to try to get at me through you – but I've got to do my duty, whatever he threatened. He must be desperate . . .'

'To hell with your duty, Stepfather – hear me out, will you?'

'Of course, lad.'

'You are not the only intended victim. If you don't care about yourself, have a care for her— '

'Her?'

'Mrs Aird. Remember his warning— '

'But why, for God's sake – what's she done?'

'Oh, that's easy – they seem to have eyes and ears, these naughty lads. They seem to know what you're both up to.'

At the glint of amusement in his stepson's eyes, Faro shuffled uncomfortably. Vince made his innocent relationship with Alison sound like an illicit *grande passion*. If only it were true.

Mrs Brook came in and began to set the table, full of apologies. She hadn't expected either of them to appear for breakfast. As she went out she beckoned to Faro from behind Vince's chair, a finger to her lips.

Faro made an excuse and followed her down to the kitchen, where he found her spreading a piece of crumpled

160

paper on the table. 'When I was putting Doctor Vince's clothes to the wash – all muddied and filthy they were, I don't know how I'll get them clean again – I found this. I thought you should maybe see it, before I gave it to the doctor, in his state.'

One glance at the note's ill-formed letters sent Faro up to his study for the anonymous note directing him to seek Clara Burnleigh's whereabouts from Mrs Wishart. Then he showed Mrs Brook's find to Vince, who read, '"Let Lily Goldie rest in peace or Mrs Aird will be next."' He threw it down on the table. 'You see? I'm telling you, take care. This isn't just your usual petty criminal working off his spite, Stepfather. Black Tam means your death.'

'I doubt whether this dire threat was penned by Black Tam's hand. Nor was it written by "One who seeks Justice".'

'I can see that. Different slant to the writing, besides the paper and ink aren't the same.' Vince frowned. 'But if Black Tam didn't put it in my pocket . . .'

'I didn't say he didn't plant it, lad, merely that he didn't write it. I'd be very surprised if he can read or write, or, even if he could, I doubt if he could spell.'

'Then who?'

'That we have still to find out.'

Vince took the note and studied it. 'You think he was paid by someone?'

'Well, there's one thing for sure. If we discover the identity of whoever wrote this, I think he's going to lead us directly to whoever murdered Lily Goldie.'

After he had eaten, Faro took the omnibus to the Central Office. He found Constable Danny McQuinn boldly sitting behind his desk, nonchalantly sorting through papers. One look at Faro's thunderous expression and McQuinn stood up, straightened his tunic, saluted smartly and said, 'I see you've been home, sir. I've been waiting most anxiously

161

to see you. It was a pity that you weren't at home when it happened.'

The implied reproof intensified Faro's own sense of guilt that while his stepson had been in mortal danger he was gallivanting about Fife, bear-leader to a crowd of irresponsible young Thespians.

He controlled his anger with difficulty. 'Perhaps you would be so good as to give me a complete report of all that happened.'

McQuinn pointed to a paper on his desk. 'It is all here, ready for you, sir.'

'I would like to hear it in your own words, McQuinn. Everything that happened.'

'I was on my normal duty-patrol in the area when I heard a man calling for help. I blew my whistle and rushed to the rescue. I used my truncheon to some effect and kept on whistling. That seemed to scare them off. At first I thought the young man on the ground was dead. He was hardly breathing and I could see in the dim light that he was in a bad way. I adopted the usual procedure of going through his pockets for identification. There was none. The light was very poor and it wasn't until I wiped some of the mud and blood from his face, which was swelling by then, that I recognised your stepson, sir.'

'There was no note in his pocket when you searched for identification?'

McQuinn shook his head. 'Nothing, sir. Nothing at all. The contents had been removed by his assailants. May I continue, sir?

'Police Constables McDonald and Scott arrived on the scene and I sent them off in pursuit of the attackers, while I carried the injured man across my shoulders to his home at Number nine Sheridan Place, where I woke up your housekeeper, Mrs Brook, who then proceeded to clean him up and dress his wounds.'

'And what did you do then?'

162

'I asked her for a pen and paper to make out a statement for Doctor Laurie to sign once he was fully conscious – for use as future evidence when the attackers were apprehended. I had a cup of tea from Mrs Brook while I waited. Doctor Laurie had come round by then and was able to give his account of the attack – signed – here. I left immediately and returned to the Central Office, where I also found Constables McDonald and Scott, who informed me that their pursuit had been unsuccessful and the robbers had vanished in the area of the Sciennes district known as the Warrens, a great place for criminals to go to earth.'

'Have you any clues to their identity?'

'Oh yes, sir. Doctor Laurie's description fitted Black Tam and his lads. As you will remember, sir,' he added proudly, 'it was Caller Jamie, his nephew, that we apprehended and put behind bars last week.'

Faro picked up Vince's statement and read it twice over, with a sense of incompleteness. There was something else about that pathetic document staring him in the face, and he just wasn't seeing it.

Across the desk was McQuinn's blandly handsome face with its suspicion of a supercilious smile. Typical of him to turn in a statement, correct in every detail, just as Vince had told him, omitting any mention of Big Tam's warning.

When he returned to Sheridan Place, Mrs Brook met him in the hall. To his question regarding Vince, she said, 'He is ever so much better now, sir. Been in his room all day, sleeping like a baby, but he managed a bowl of porridge. A wee touch of yon powder works wonders. I hear that even Her Majesty approves of laudanum and has a supply of it when she stays up at Balmoral.' Mrs Brook's awed whisper implied a guarantee of unquestionable respectability.

'Have there been any visitors?'

'Yes, Inspector. Mrs Aird called in before going to the theatre. She left a message that she would return later in

163

the hope of seeing you.' At that moment the sound of the front doorbell jangled through the hall.

'That'll be her now, sir. Shall I send her up?'

'If you please.'

He heard her light step on the stairs and she ran into the room and, rushing over to him, threw her arms about his neck. She was trembling. 'Jeremy, my dear, I am so relieved to see you. What a day I have put in. Something rather awful happened when I got back to Mrs Penny's. This!' From her reticule she took out an envelope addressed 'Mrs Aird'. 'It was waiting for me. Read it.'

In the same ill-formed letters, on identical paper to the note Vince had received, was the warning, 'Let Lily Goldie rest in peace and go back where you belong if you want to stay alive.'

'Jeremy, I'm afraid. I don't know any Lily Goldie. What are they talking about?'

'Lily Goldie is the girl from the convent— '

'You mean – you mean the one who – who was murdered?' He saw now how afraid she was, as her voice rose shrilly. 'Oh my God, how dreadful. But what has that to do with me?'

He put his arm around her trembling shoulders. 'Not a thing, my dear. It just happens that I'm carrying on a private investigation – on behalf of relatives . . .'

'Wait a moment – of course, that was why you were going to Fairmilehead – when you took me with you.'

'Yes.'

She looked at him wild-eyed. 'But that had nothing to do with me. I wasn't helping you – I hardly knew you— '

'My dear, please be calm.'

'Calm!'

'I'll explain everything, but tell me first, when did you receive this?'

'Mrs Penny said it must have been handed in some time when I was out on Sunday. See – there's no postage stamp.'

164

'Doesn't Mrs Penny remember who . . .?'

Alison shook her head. 'The usual thing is for the postman or anyone leaving messages to put them on the table in the lobby. The front door is never locked, so it might have been delivered any time.'

'When did you last receive any mail?'

She frowned. 'I occasionally receive letters from admirers – you know, the kind actresses get – and that is all. We all pick up our letters from the lobby table as we come in. Jeremy, what does it mean? Who would write such a beastly note?'

'Tell me about the other boarders.'

'Only the girls from the theatre, Beth, Marie, Julia – oh yes, and Hugo. He moved in last week, some trouble with his landlady's family arriving, and Mrs Penny agreed to put him in the attic, temporarily.'

She looked at Faro earnestly. 'You can't possibly think – I mean, its unimaginable – the girls are a terrible tease, but they mean no harm. And none of these dear young people are capable of playing such cruel and frightening practical jokes.'

'I'm afraid this is no practical joke.'

'You mean – it is serious, someone is threatening me, just because I happened – quite innocently – to go with you to Fairmilehead? But that is monstrous, monstrous – it's so unfair – oh, dear God . . .' Alison sat down, her face pale. 'What will they do to me?'

'Nothing. I shall look after you. I mean it.' Faro poured out a cup of tea. 'Here you are. Go on, drink it. Do as I tell you.' He drew up a chair opposite, and, scrutinising the letter lying between them on the table, said, 'Vince received a similar threat. By the same hand, I'd say, and in almost the same words.'

'When was this?'

'Mrs Brook discovered it when she was attending to his clothes. It had been thrust into his coat pocket.'

165

'I still don't understand.'

'I think I'm beginning to – it fits a definite pattern, although I wouldn't have expected it quite so soon.'

'Pattern? What pattern are you talking about?'

'Someone is getting very anxious about our interest in Lily Goldie's murder.'

Alison frowned. 'I don't understand. Wasn't a man hanged – dreadful case, he murdered someone else, didn't he?' She shook her head, trying to remember.

'His wife. However, we have uncovered evidence which leads us to believe that in fact the man who was hanged – Hymes – was innocent of Lily Goldie's murder.'

Alison stared at him. 'Are you saying that there is another murderer still on the loose?'

'I'm afraid so, and he realises – somehow – that we are catching up with him. That is why he is getting desperate, trying to scare us with threats. Have no doubt, my dear, that whoever wrote these two notes is our man. And I mean to get him, and he knows that. Now, I will see you safe back to your lodging and take the opportunity of making a few enquiries.'

'No, please, Jeremy, I don't want Mrs Penny involved and the girls frightened – a murderer on the loose! And Mrs Penny has been so good to me, and now I've brought this terror to her door. I beg you – please don't . . .'

'I'm sorry, I have to do it, my dear. I have to follow up the attack on my stepson and every shred of evidence.'

Hearing them coming downstairs, Vince emerged from his bedroom. Apart from the angry-looking bruises his appearance was considerably better than Faro had expected.

Alison ran to him with a little cry and put her arms around him. Again this display of maternal concern and affection moved Faro deeply. Vince liked her. She would have made a splendid stepmother.

'May I show him the letter?' she said.

Vince read it and whistled. 'You too? That's jolly

166

interesting. Handed in to Mrs Penny's, you say? Well, Stepfather, where do we go from here?'

'"We" don't go anywhere, lad. I think it would be better if I worked alone from now on and didn't involve either you or Mrs Aird.'

Vince sighed. 'If you must, but I do enjoy playing detective – and I have some ideas of my own I would like to put to the test.'

'You take care,' said Faro sternly. 'I don't want any repetitions of last night's misadventure.' And to Alison, 'Let us go now. Rest assured I shall be very tactful with Mrs Penny. You may rely on me not to make it sound like a police investigation.'

Vince waved to them from the window, and Alison blew him a kiss. Closing the gate, she sighed, 'Such a dear boy. Tell me, why doesn't he just call you Father? Or Jeremy, for that matter?'

'Never Jeremy. He wouldn't consider that quite proper.'

'But you are such friends.'

'That has not always been so. When I first knew him, as a little boy, it was Mr Faro. But from the day his mother and I married, he called me Stepfather. And I must confess I rather like the title, seeing that it is perfectly accurate and it makes it somehow special.'

They found Mrs Penny in the garden attending to the roses. She greeted them both effusively and when Mrs Aird went indoors was quite disposed to linger and chat with Inspector Faro, waxing voluble in response to his warnings about a spate of petty thievings from unguarded kitchens in the area, and the necessity of locking the door at night, at least until the criminals were apprehended.

'I've already been warned, Inspector. Constable McQuinn was saying the same things when I found him in my kitchen on Sunday.' She smiled slyly. 'Mind you, I thought it was maybe a wee bit of an excuse – I think Bessie, the pretty little maid I've engaged to help me with the washing, is the reason for his particular interest in these premises.'

'What other callers have you had recently?'

'Apart from Doctor Laurie – he was worried about you all missing the ferry . . .' She hesitated, her smile inviting explanation.

'I mean strangers, Mrs Penny, during the last few days.'

'Oh well, let me see now. On Saturday, there were two wee lads selling firewood, an old beggarman, the minister. And on Sunday, if you please, Inspector, a gypsy woman, selling clothes pegs and telling fortunes. Well, I sent her packing, such wickedness on the Lord's day. I didn't like the look of her.' She frowned. 'She was filthy, Inspector. In fact, I wondered if she could be a woman, she had this long stringy black hair and I thought her hands and feet were rather big and her voice a wee bit on the deep side.'

'You thought she might be a man, eh?' said Faro, thinking here was a stroke of luck.

Mrs Penny nodded vigorously. 'I did indeed. She came just as we were leaving for church, too. What a cheek . . .'

Faro escaped with difficulty and made his way to the Central Office.

'Is there anything on Black Tam yet?' he asked McQuinn, eyeing with disapproval the pipe that the young constable was smoking, since this was a privilege only allowed to senior officers and detectives.

'Nothing yet, Inspector. But do give us time – it's early days, as you know from your own experience.'

Faro shrugged irritably. McQuinn never missed an opportunity of reminding him that once upon a time he too had been a humble policeman doing duty-patrol in the streets of Edinburgh.

'What about routine enquiries in the area?'

McQuinn produced a long list and Faro felt, instead of gratification, annoyance that his efficiency could not be faulted.

'What about Mrs Penny at Marchmont Cottage?'

'Mrs Penny? There was no reason to enquire at her house. The attack wasn't in her vicinity.'

'And yet you went there on Sunday.'

McQuinn blushed. 'Oh, that! Nothing to do with official enquiries, Inspector. I was merely paying court to the pretty little lass in the kitchen. And when Mrs Penny caught us, I felt obliged to make an excuse for my presence,' he added with a smirk that infuriated Faro.

'Indeed, Constable. You might endeavour in future to keep your private life separate from your police duties. It would be a great help. In connection with the attack on my stepson, you might keep a lookout for a tall gypsy woman with uncommon large feet and hands and a be-grimed appearance.'

'You think it might be Black Tam in disguise?'

'Never mind what I think, Constable, and I will be obliged if you will keep your eyes open when you are on duty, less in the region of kitchen-maids and more in the region of possible suspects.'

In the days that followed, there were no more threatening notes or suspicious incidents. With the healthy flesh of youth, Vince's bruises and cuts healed and he had almost forgotten his attack in his excitement about Mrs Penny's mysterious gypsy visitor.

'I'm absolutely certain that she – or more probably he – is responsible for leaving the note for Mrs Aird. Find him, Stepfather, and we have the man we're looking for – Lily Goldie's murderer.'

Faro was inclined to share his enthusiasm, especially as neither McQuinn nor any of the other constables alerted found a trace or a hint of the existence of the gypsy, who had apparently vanished into thin air since the visit to Marchmont Cottage.

There was still the business of Vince's threatening note, which McQuinn swore was not in his pockets when he searched them in Gibbet Lane. That and the fact that McQuinn had also visited Mrs Penny's that Sunday were matters that needed careful and tactful investigation, considering that he had also been 'sweet' on Lily Goldie.

And why should Black Tam be concerned with the murdered girl? None of it made any sense.

Faro now had his own reasons for personal anxiety, which tended to make him less enthusiastic or vigilant about following clues to the identity of the second murderer. In a few days, the Trelawney Thespians – and Alison – would be gone from Edinburgh. At least she would be safe from any vengeful attacks. He had already made up his mind, despite her protests, not to let her go out of his life for ever. No one who had made such an impact on his senses could say goodbye and walk away.

Soon, too, he would be once more involved in domesticity, in his sorely neglected role of father to his two daughters. A letter lay on his desk from Orkney.

Dearest Papa,
    We are looking forward to being all together again, with our dear brother Vince, in your new house in Edinburgh, as you promised. We hope you will like the enclosed which Granny says is a good likeness . . .

He looked at the smiling photograph and it made him acutely aware of time passing. How they had grown – soon they would be young ladies and he would have lost their childhood.

He groaned as he re-read the letter. '. . . as you promised' reproached him. He had forgotten, or rather pushed it to the back of his mind. However, unless the mystery of the threatening letters was solved and Lily Goldie's murderer apprehended and safe behind bars, he felt the presence of any other members of his family would be an added hazard.

170

Already he was wary of providing Vince with any additional information that might lead him recklessly to follow 'clues' on his own with disastrous, and this time perhaps fatal, results.

Faro knew of only one way to resolve his difficulties, and that was to set a police trap. Vince listened gravely to his plan.

'You might as well know, Stepfather, I can't stop you but I'm against it. It's far too dangerous. Take care, you may have gone too far this time and played into the murderer's hands.'

CHAPTER FIFTEEN

That Saturday night was brilliantly moon-lit. As midnight chimed from a vast number of distant Edinburgh churches solemnly proclaiming the Sabbath morn, a white-haired bearded old gentleman wearing a silk-lined cape, top hat and carrying an elegant cane was seen to leave the neighbourhood of the King's Theatre. Merrily, but somewhat unsteadily, he proceeded along Lothian Road and across the Meadows, heading towards the new villas by the short cut at Gibbet Lane.

If any had remarked upon his passing it would have been to the effect that he would have been wiser to hire a cab. Elderly, crippled in the left leg, his progress was further impeded by the condition of one who has imbibed too well. The further he walked, the slower and the more pronounced his limp. Now a shortness of breath, a wheezing cough, added to the picture of decrepitude as he stopped frequently, leaning on his cane.

The onlooker would have further decided that a man, obviously wealthy, was not quite in his right mind to choose such exercise at his time of life when he was so out of condition, as he disappeared from view along the tree-lined lane. But the path was deserted – or so it seemed to the limping man, when suddenly, from behind the trees, three masked men, two of average height and one very large, leaped out at him.

The old man cried out 'Help!' in a voice surprisingly

strong, and even as they descended upon him his bent back straightened and from the cane appeared a fine-bladed sword which flashed in the moonlight as, with limp miraculously cured, he turned upon his assailants.

'Scarper!'

The leader's warning came too late. The old man was using a whistle to ear-piercing effect and from every tree policemen erupted, racing down upon them. In the lead was Constable Danny McQuinn, who, for once, Faro was extremely glad to see.

'A nice piece of work, Inspector. You make a very convincing old man, to the life – as if it was yourself only without the beard.'

Faro wasn't sure what to make of this enigmatic remark but chose, for once, to take it as flattery. 'Put them on a charge and keep them inside. Send someone to get my stepson to identify them.'

Black Tam and his associates were bundled into a cab and escorted to the Central Office. Dr Laurie was at home. Presented with his stepfather's compliments, he was hustled into the second cab.

'What's this all about? Where is Inspector Faro?' he demanded, confronted by the back of the elderly gentleman still in his disguise and whom he failed to recognise in the dim light.

'Why, Stepfather! Your plan worked after all.'

'Come with me, lad.'

A look into the cell and Vince said, 'Oh yes, those are the three who attacked me right enough.'

'Good! You can formally bring charges, then. See the Constable and he'll tell you what's needed. The cab will take you back home.'

'Aren't you coming too?'

'I may be a little while. Goodnight, lad. See you in the morning.'

Faro then confronted Black Tam and his two bullies,

and charged them with assault. 'You know who I am?'

'God perhaps, with that white beard,' said Big Tam sourly.

'It would pay you to be serious.' And Faro removed his disguise, while watching carefully Black Tam's reactions.

'A copper as I live an' breathe,' was the sneering response. 'I might ha' kenned as much.'

'You know me.'

'I do?'

'My name is Inspector Faro.'

'That's a funny name for a copper.'

'It might be a very significant name in your case, my lad. I suspect that you've already heard it.'

'Never. And I don't want to hear it no more, neither.'

'Listen, Tam – I can make it easier for you, if you co-operate. Who paid you to leave a note in Doctor Laurie's pocket when you robbed him the other night?'

Black Tam stared at him blankly. 'Do me a favour, Inspector. Don't know what you're on about. What would I be doing putting things into folks' pockets? Goes against the grain, that does. Opposite is what I'm at – taking things out, as you ken fine well.' He grinned.

'Do you know an old gypsy woman – about your height, with large hands and feet, who sells clothes-pegs and tells fortunes?'

'Never heard of her.'

'You don't know anything of a visit she made to Mrs Penny at Marchmont Cottage, and delivered a note there?'

Big Tam shook his great head from side to side. 'You're talking double-dutch, Inspector.' And, appealing to the silent Constable McQuinn, 'What's he on about the now?'

And Faro felt uneasily that unless Big Tam was an extremely good actor, which he doubted, then he was telling the truth.

'You maintain that you've never seen me before?'

174

'Never. Heard plenty about ye, kenned you was a copper to be avoided, but never been my misfortune to set eyes on ye afore.'

'I also happen to be Doctor Laurie's stepfather.'

With elaborate casualness, the man replied, 'Is that a fact? Well now, wasn't it just ma bad luck to choose a lad who was copper's kin?' He spat on the floor. 'An' all for a miserable two shillings.'

'Read him the charge, Constable, the attack on Doctor Laurie.'

Big Tam listened and shuffled his feet.

'Have you anything you wish to say that might be used in evidence?'

'Don't know my own strength, Inspector. Used to be a wrestler before I fell on hard times.'

'Like robbery with violence. I believe you are also part of a conspiracy— '

'I ain't part of nothing. Work for meself, I do. Only rob the rich to give to the poor.'

'Sit down – here at the desk.'

Black Tam regarded him nervously. 'What for?'

'Because I tell you to. Go on.'

Faro produced the two notes, the one found on Vince and the one to Alison Aird.

'Here is paper. Take up that pen . . .'

Black Tam held the pen, rolling it between his fingers. 'What's it about, Inspector. What's your game?'

'I want you to write something for me. Your name, for instance.'

The pen scratched long and laboriously. 'Thos Macandlish. That's me name.'

'Now let's have your address.'

'Haven't got one.'

'Central Office, Edinburgh. That will find you for some time to come.'

In answer, Tam drew a large and shaky cross under his

175

signature. Looking over his shoulder, Faro said, 'What's this? I thought you could write?'

Black Tam grinned sheepishly. 'Only me name – learned it by heart lang syne. Was told it would be useful, but I canna write anything else, honest to God, mister.'

'Maybe you can read then?' And Faro thrust the note in front of him. Black Tam looked at it solemnly and shook his head.

'Dunno what it says. Never learned letters, only numbers. I can read numbers,' he said helpfully.

'Take them to the cells,' said Faro in disgust.

There was not the slightest resemblance in Tam's shaky signature to the firm educated hand of the notes, and Faro was more than ever convinced that he was looking at the writing of the man who had murdered Lily Goldie. To his mind there were four classes of murderer. The once-only murderer who, of a violent disposition, often combined with poor mental powers, comes home and finds his woman in bed with another man. He picks up the nearest implement and murders her – and often her lover as well. There is no subtlety involved. He might make a run for it, but most often when his blood-lust has cooled, and he slowly realises the enormity of his action, his run is not away from the scene of the crime but to the nearest police station to give himself up. And even if he tries to escape the law, his getaway is usually easy to follow. He leaves plenty of clues. Almost as if he wanted to be found. Such a murderer was Hymes.

In the second category was the mad murderer, driven to kill for pleasure, or wreaking his revenge on society for some imagined wrong, working out of his system some ancient grievance that had twisted his mind. Prostitutes were their most common prey. Such mass-murderers often evaded the law by the use of cunning and ingenuity. However, they were rarely encountered, thought Faro, thankfully.

176

The third was the poisoner, the man or woman driven beyond all endurance, or by lust, loathing or lucre, to get rid of the impediment to what they imagined was peace, often accompanied by plenty. It rarely worked and, unless they had a considerable run of luck, they were most often caught and hanged.

The first-category murderer was often violent and ignorant, the two latter were considerably more wily and intelligent. So too the fourth and last, the man who employed a bully, a strong man with poor reasoning, 'bought' for the purpose of committing murder or to intimidate the chosen victim. Such as Black Tam, disguised as a gypsy woman, delivering warning notes. No, it was too far-fetched.

So, in which category did Lily Goldie's murderer belong? Once he had reasoned that out, he would be much nearer to his goal. But somewhere, he realised, he had lost the track. There was a great muddle of clues, and none of them made any sense at all.

Again and again he returned to the two notes. Although the writing was doubtless disguised, it was definitely that of an educated hand.

Once again the tide of thefts, assaults, embezzlements and arson took over. As Faro dealt with the routine investigations he hoped fervently that no major crime would erupt on Edinburgh society and cause him to miss the Trelawney Thespians' farewell performance of *Antony and Cleopatra*, and his last evening with Alison before her departure for Bournemouth.

He returned from the Central Office to be met in the hall by Mrs Brook, who handed a note to him.

'Will you please remember to give this to Mrs Aird at the next opportunity?' At his blank look, she said, 'It is a recipe for my pancakes which I promised her. They were greatly enjoyed by those young actresses and it is a recipe they can make themselves. It is quite simple. I would have

177

entrusted it to Doctor Vince, but he is so forgetful— '

Faro cut short the tirade with solemn promises and hurried up to his study and closed the door.

His desk was awash with papers and, carefully laying aside Mrs Brook's recipe, he decided that with the impending visit from Orkney, he must placate the housekeeper by a brisk attempt at tidiness. His study was a constant affront to her sense of order and she insisted that before the family visit the room, from which her activities were normally barred, must be thoroughly cleansed.

The bright sunshine through the window revealed very clearly, even to his undomestic eye, the source of Mrs Brook's anguish. Most of his desk was presently occupied by evidence relating to Lily Goldie's murder. Glad that the case was now finally closed, even if unsolved, he took out a large packet and gathered all the documents together. On top were the two warning notes received by Alison and Vince, which had led to his decision to abandon the investigation.

A sudden shaft of sunlight also took in Mrs Brook's pancake recipe. Faro snatched it up with a surge of excitement. Why on earth had he not noticed that before?

Taking out the two warning notes, he laid the new note alongside.

For a moment he sat back in his chair, dazed with certain knowledge that he had found what he had been looking for. That elusive link, something his acute sense of observation recognised but which lay dormant, nagging him, below the surface of his mind.

He rushed downstairs to the kitchen where Mrs Brook was rolling pastry for an apple pie and, flourishing the recipe, he said, 'Have you any more of this paper, Mrs Brook?'

Somewhat guiltily, he thought, she went to a drawer and withdrew several sheets. 'Here it is, sir. That's all that's left.'

'Where did it come from?' And examining it closely, he said, 'You've cut something off the top, Mrs Brook.'

'Yes, I did, sir. But how did you know?'

'Your scissors need sharpening, their cutting edge is rough.'

'I might as well tell truth, sir, this paper belonged to the late doctor. Seemed a wicked waste to throw it away, with his name printed on it and all. So after he passed on, I decided to use it up for my recipes. Did I do wrong, sir?' she asked anxiously.

'Of course not. Such economies are admirable, Mrs Brook. But, may I ask, where did the ink come from?'

'Oh, the doctor had his ink specially prepared. Very fussy about it clotting when he was writing out his pre-scriptions.'

'So you've been using up the bottle.'

'Yes, sir. It's rather thick now, not the kind you would want.'

Faro sat down at the table. 'Mrs Brook, can you tell me who had access to this paper – apart from yourself – in recent weeks?'

Mrs Brook thought for a moment. 'Nobody – that is, except Constable McQuinn. That night when Doctor Vince was brought home. He wanted to write out a state-ment for the poor lad to sign. I was that flustered and upset, sir, I just gave him what came to hand.'

Faro took a gig to the Central Office and extracted McQuinn's handwritten statement regarding Black Tam. Leaving a message for the Constable to meet him at the Pleasance Theatre at seven o'clock, he returned home. As he expected, the two warning notes and Vince's statement had all been written in identical ink, with the same pen on identical paper with a jagged edge.

But not in the same hand. And he knew he had solved Lily Goldie's murder. The thought gave him no satisfaction as even now, reluctant to believe what he knew to be true,

179

he spread the notes out on his study table, pushing aside the smiling photograph of his two small daughters.

For himself, at that moment, he could see no future beyond the next few hours. How long he sat wrestling with his conscience, he did not know, hardly aware in his anguish that Vince had come in and was regarding his slumped shoulders, his downbent head with compassion.

'Stepfather? What is it?'

Faro wearily handed him the three notes, and described the events of the last few hours. 'We've solved the case. Haven't you guessed, Vince lad?'

Vince sat down opposite. 'This lets out the Mad Bart, doesn't it? And McQuinn,' he said, comparing the handwriting. 'We've eliminated everyone else. Except . . .'

'Except?'

'The schoolboy. Yes, it has to be him.'

'A schoolboy who never existed. Except to murder Lily Goldie.'

'Therefore it had to be someone acting the part of a schoolboy.' Vince smiled wanly. 'And as soon as you put the words "acting the part" into context, everything else falls into shape.'

'It was Hugo who gave us the answer, yet neither of us could see it.'

'We didn't want to see it.'

'Dear God, I don't want to see it now, staring me in the face.'

Vince laid a hand on his shoulder. 'What will you do, Stepfather? You can't mean . . .'

Faro stood up, buttoned his coat. 'Lad, I can and do mean just that. And I need you as witness. Will you do this for me?'

And, aware of his stepson's appalled expression, he went out, closed the door behind him and set off for the Pleasance Theatre.

CHAPTER SIXTEEN

He found Alison in her dressing-room. He knew she would be alone as the make-up for Cleopatra took some time.

The mask of beauty took his breath away. How skilfully before his eyes the Queen of the Nile, she whom age could not wither, nor custom stale, was coming to life, as the short, red-gold curls disappeared beneath the heavy Egyptian headdress.

'Don't hover, Jeremy. Take a seat, please. You can talk to me while I put on the finishing touches.'

He sat down heavily, his resolve shattered. Yet there were so many indisputable facts. If his emotional involvement had not blinded him, he would have recognised them immediately. Smiling, she regarded him through the mirror. 'You're looking so solemn, Jeremy. I've promised to be your friend and I will write to you, if that is what you would like. So do cheer up, we want our last evening to be merry.'

Merry, he thought. Would he ever be merry again?

'I have something to tell you.'

'Oh, something nice, I hope.'

'Not nice. Something very serious.'

'Oh?' She swung round to face him. 'And what is that?'

Trying to keep his voice and emotions under control, he said, 'I want you to tell me how you lured Lily Goldie up to Salisbury Crags by pretending to be Tim Ferris's schoolboy brother. We believe you then pushed her over the edge and knotted a scarf about her neck to make it look like the work of Patrick Hymes.'

The make-up was too thick for him to see if she paled at this accusation, but it was a little while before she asked quietly, 'You have proof?'

She did not deny it. Oh dear God, why didn't she deny it, laugh at him?

'You wrote these, didn't you?'

She merely glanced at the notes he held out but made no attempt to examine them. Had she been innocent, she would have snatched them from him with cries of indignation. Had she been innocent . . . but she merely smiled.

'You are clever. You must tell me where I went wrong.'

'First, your reluctance to be seen as a boy, in your Portia costume. You almost slammed the dressing-room door in my face.'

She shrugged. 'I was tired. I had been on stage for hours. Perhaps I do not like being seen by men alone in my dressing-room, "showing off my limbs" as I seem to remember Beth called it.'

'Actresses have no such modesty, as well you know. The girls at Vince's party assured us that you made a splendid boy, and yet you refused to appear with them as one of the young gentlemen from Venice.'

Still she smiled but, watching her, he repeated Hugo's mocking words. '"Some squeaking Cleopatra boy my greatness . . ." '

Her lips moved, but no words came and he remembered that other time, her startled look which he had interpreted as embarrassment, was fear, deadly fear.

'Are you going to arrest me?' she asked lightly and went back to looking in the mirror. How could she sound so casual, uninterested even? Faro realised he had not thought that far ahead. He went to the door.

'Come in, Vince. McQuinn, you take a seat – over there.'

And to Alison, 'Mrs Aird, you are charged with the murder of Lily Goldie – for God's sake, woman, why?' His voice shook and, fighting for control, he added quietly, 'It might make it easier for you if, in your statement, you have good reasons.'

What nonsense, he thought. Nothing would change. They would hang his Desdemona, whatever her excuse. Hang her by that lovely slender neck until she was dead. He wanted to rush from the room, fly from the inevitable, but he was aware of Vince's hand heavy on his shoulder.

'How did you convince her to go with you, Mrs Aird?'

Alison looked at Vince, smiling, and then stared across at McQuinn as if puzzled by his presence, and then with a shrug, she said, 'It was quite simple. Her natural greed. I told her that Tim had left in my keeping, at St Leonard's, a large package for her, just before he – he walked under the train. I indicated that I was certain it contained money and items of valuable family jewellery. That brought her out, faster than summer lightning.' She shrugged. 'The rest was easy. That isolated path, no one around so early. I told her, "I have a nice surprise for you. Close your eyes and hold out your hands." '

Faro shuddered at the suddenly boyish treble. She must have had no trouble deceiving anyone. 'But your reason? I suppose Tim Ferris was your lover, was that it – jealousy?'

'Tim – my lover?' She laughed, and then turned her head away and looked at Vince, a long, tender appraisal. 'Not my lover. Tim was my son.'

'Your son?'

'My son, my only child, and she destroyed him as readily as if her hands had pushed him to his death. She deserved to die. I knew that and I was determined that if I couldn't make her feel the horror of being pushed under a train, at least she would know the full horror of violent death, of being pushed from a great height— '

'Tim was your son?'

'Timon, I called him, after *Timon of Athens*, the play I was in in London when I met his father. Oh, his father was so like him in looks, and, alas, in nature. A handsome plausible rogue who couldn't resist wine, women and a more than occasional flutter on the gaming tables. He married me because it was the only way he could get me into his bed, persuade me to leave the theatre. I was seventeen. Everyone said I was a fool to give up a promising career, but I didn't mind. Marrying him was a triumph and I was blissfully happy – for a little while. Happy as I shall never again be in this life.'

Her face darkened. 'Then, one day when I was pregnant, a woman came to see me with three young children. One glance at them, and she didn't need to tell me that they were his. She handed me a marriage certificate. She was Julian Aird's wife and I was bigamously married. She was determined on vengeance and he was still in prison when Timon was born.'

She clasped her hands. 'Timon was the most beautiful baby. I loved him, he was my whole world, and I could hardly bear to let him out of my sight. I gave up all hope of being an actress until he was older. I was determined that he should have the life he would have had if Julian had really been my husband. I found a rich protector – I'm not ashamed – a dear elderly man who was my lover. He died when Tim was eight years old and left me all his fortune.

'Then, one day, I decided to tell Tim the truth. That the man he regarded as his father was my lover. That I wasn't a widow and that he was illegitimate.'

She stopped, and even through the make-up he saw the tragedy lurking in her eyes. 'He never forgave me. He was a child still but he called me terrible – filthy – names. It was dreadful, but I knew how I had hurt him. He was broken-hearted, so ashamed of the awful stigma I had branded him with. We were living in Yorkshire, in a lovely country mansion, but he had always wanted to go to Scotland. I had told him so much about it. I decided to send him to boarding school in Edinburgh, to St Leonard's. So far away from me, but I hoped that one day when he was older he would understand that everything I had done was for his sake, for his future. Then I set up the trust fund, put every penny into it, so that he could enjoy a good life. I went back to the stage and tried to work with Scottish companies, so that I could be near him.

'I hardly ever saw him. Going back to the stage made matters worse – a mother who was an actress, as well as a kept whore. He did not want to see me in Edinburgh. I thought it would be different when he went to medical school. He would be a man then, he would understand about life. But time made matters worse. He made excuses not to meet me, forbade me to visit his lodgings. When we did meet, he would hardly spend time to speak to me. Then, early this year, I saw a new side of him, besotted with this girl who was out to ruin him. Now all he wanted from me was more and more money, to buy her trinkets, to persuade her that he was a rich man who wanted to marry her. It wasn't until he failed his qualifying exams that I learned – from his own lips – that he had gambled away the entire trust fund that remained on this woman. And when it was all spent, she wanted no more of him.

'Even then I didn't realise how much he loved her. I couldn't believe that anyone could make him suffer so much that he would walk under a railway train. He did so, without a moment's consideration of what I might suffer as his mother,' she added harshly. 'Not one thought as to my agonies, a fine end to all my sacrifices and devotion. I had given up everything for him, a stage career as a Shakespearean actress – I mean a real one – on the London stage, not this absurd company.

'Now it was this woman's turn to suffer and I was determined to destroy her. But how? Then one day, when I was out walking, I found a St Leonard's cap on the railings. Some boy had dropped it. I knew I made a convincing boy – I could convince her, strike up an acquaintance as Tim's heart-broken young brother. She was flattered that a schoolboy should seek her out, pay court to her.

'Soon I saw the perfect opportunity to destroy her. The murder of Sarah Hymes. I could make it look like a double murder.' She laughed. 'You know, I never realised that murder could be so easy. I went back a few times afterwards, hung about the convent gates. That took some courage, just to be seen as a lovesick schoolboy grieving.'

'So that you would never be suspected. And you succeeded.'

She looked at him sadly. 'When I first met you, you seemed determined to fall in love with me, so I felt quite safe, even though I did have occasional qualms. I knew you were clever and I didn't think I could fool you for ever, which was why I was determined to keep you at arm's length. Yet luck was always with me. Even the night you were attacked, Vince.'

She swung round and faced him for the first time. 'I was so fond of him,' she said to Faro. 'He reminded me of my own son, the same age, both studying medicine in the same year.'

Faro exchanged a startled glance with Vince, for the parallels were even closer. Both were illegitimate, both fighting the stigma of bastardy.

'It was because I was so concerned about your toothache, poor suffering darling, that I came to your house and succumbed to the temptation of planting the two notes. It seemed such a perfect chance to plant some evidence that pointed to his attackers. And if I received a warning, who then could possibly suspect me? I'd seen Mrs Brook take out paper and ink in the kitchen to give to the Constable.'

186

'That was your fatal mistake. I might never have guessed, if you hadn't used that special notepaper.'

She shrugged. 'How was I to know? I thought all paper and ink were the same. And now, Inspector – what are you going to do with me? I presume that the Constable is here to arrest me?'

When he didn't reply, she sighed. 'I have one request. In Desdemona's immortal words, "Kill me tomorrow, but let me live tonight." Will you ask him to do that for me, Vince?' And, turning to Faro she said, 'Please, Jeremy, because you loved me once.'

Because I still love you – desperately, were the words he longed to say and could not.

'My last Cleopatra. The Constable may sit outside the dressing-room, quite discreetly.' She gave him a flashing smile. 'I won't run away. You have my word. Besides,' she added, looking wistfully across at Vince, as if seeing in him again the son she had lost, 'there is no place to run to any more. Without love, there isn't very much worth having in a woman's world.'

Or in mine. Oh my dearest . . .

Outside her dressing-room, McQuinn took a seat. 'You go to the front, sir, just in case. I'll stay here, at that rate we'll have both exits covered.'

Vince was waiting for him in the green-room and handed him a large brandy. 'Drink it, Stepfather. You look so ill.'

'I feel ill. If finding out the woman you love is a murderess can count as illness, then I feel like death.'

'What about her? Will you let her carry on with the performance?'

'Yes. I don't see why not. There won't be much theatre where she's going,' he added grimly.

'Has it got to be . . .?' Vince shrugged. 'Tim was so unworthy of her. I never liked him, but what a brute. How could he have treated his mother like that, especially one so sweet and loving.'

'We will never know his reasons now, that's for sure.'

'Quite candidly, one could almost be glad he's dead. He and the Goldie woman. The world's a cleaner place without either of them.' Pausing, he looked at Faro. 'You realise she's not quite sane, don't you, driven mad by his cruelty. If ever there was a *crime passionnel*, this was it.'

'We'd have a hard job convincing the judges.'

'Surely you'll do your best, try for manslaughter?'

'Oh God, Vince lad, don't ask me. Not just now.'

The bell rang for curtain up and they stood at the back, but neither had much concentration left for the play which now enthralled and held its audience captive for the last time.

Between the acts, the green-room was filled with noisy enthusiastic students, and with nothing left to say, Faro and Vince walked outside. They stood gazing up at Arthur's Seat with a pale moon rising, although the sky was still cloudless and blue. A warm, windless, seductively romantic night, but for Faro its beauty merely mocked his agony.

Vince took his arm. 'I think, Stepfather, that we've always known there was something like this. I didn't want to face it.' He looked at the scene before them thoughtfully. 'Remember the night I was attacked, and she stayed, afraid to go home?'

'What happened?'

'I was half asleep, dozing, but I thought – I thought I saw her turn up the lamp and slip something into my coat pocket. Then she picked up paper and ink from the table, as if she had been writing, and carried them out of the door, looking over to where I lay. There was something about her manner, very nervous and furtive. Of course, I'd been so knocked about, I could have been slightly delirious, and next day, when I learned that she too had received a warning note, I decided that I had dreamed the whole thing.'

188

They heard the bell for the last act. 'It's turning cold, let's go inside, Stepfather.' At the door, he said desperately, 'Look, can't you possibly let her go, pretend none of this ever happened? They're leaving Edinburgh tomorrow.'

'Vince lad, I can't, and you know I can't. My whole faith in myself, in my job – and in justice being done – would be gone for ever if I did. I might as well crawl into a hole, for I'd never live with myself again.'

'And yet the demands of justice have been met. The case is closed.'

Faro felt chilled to the heart. 'Morally, that makes no difference. There is a murderer going free, however you choose to interpret it.'

There were no seats available, but from where they stood near the front they could see the stage plainly, with McQuinn and two uniformed reinforcements hovering discreetly in the wings.

Cleopatra's death scene was played before a hushed audience, that lovely bell-like voice echoing, holding the playgoers spellbound. For them, Edinburgh had vanished, the greasepaint, the over-acting of Antony and the supporting cast was forgotten. This was Egypt and Cleopatra was about to die by her own hand.

> 'Give me my robe, put on my crown; I have
> Immortal longings in me . . .
> . . . Husband, I come . . .
> I am fire and air; my other elements
> I give to baser life . . .
> Come then, and take the last warmth of my lips.
> Farewell, kind Charmain – Iras, long farewell.'

Beth, as Iras, reeled dramatically and fell with a mighty groan. Cleopatra knelt beside her, regarded her tenderly.

> 'Have I the aspic in my lips? Dost fall?'

Again a mighty groan and writhing on the floor announced that Iras was loathe to lose this dramatic moment, despite Cleopatra's comment,

'If thou and nature can so gently part,
The stroke of death is as a lover's pinch,
Which hurts and is desir'd . . .'

Faro watched as she took the asp, saw the red jewels that were its eyes glint and flash fire. He stood transfixed, unable to believe that this was Alison Aird, a confessed murderess, and not the Queen of the Nile, Shakespeare's 'lass unparallel'd' as he listened to the dying words, saw the asp's bright jewels plunge.

'What, should I stay— '

And then she fell, not back on her funeral couch to lie there regal and dignified. Instead, she jerked once, like a puppet, and slithered to the floor. Her last words were lost as Charmain screamed out loud and the curtain descended abruptly to tumultuous cheering.

Now the audience were on their feet. They began to applaud wildly, stamping feet, unaware apparently that the play was not yet over. Where were the guards and Dolabella and Caesar's entry and triumphant oration?

There was something wrong. Vince took one look at his stepfather and began to struggle through the cheering students. There was movement on stage, a great hush. But it was only Antony. Antony without Cleopatra at his side, who staggered forward and looked somewhat ashen-faced under his make-up.

Trembling, he held up his hand for silence. His plea was ignored; the stamping, cheering began again.

'Cleopatra. We want Cleopatra.'

'We want Mrs Aird, Mrs Aird.'

The stage-hands, unaware of any disaster, set in motion the machinery. Antony's shout – 'Keep the curtain lowered, for God's sake' – came too late.

The curtain rose slowly to reveal Cleopatra lying where she had fallen. It was no ornamental asp at her breast, but the jewelled dagger, embedded to its hilt, and the dark red on her white robe grew to a monstrous rose, as slowly her lifeblood seeped away. It ran, a thin red line, flowing unevenly across the boards to where Faro, with Vince at his side, was already leaping on to the stage.